# THE
# CHICKEN BONE
# WISH

(hardcover title: Joshua, the Czar, and the Chicken Bone Wish)

by
## Barbara Girion

Illustrated by
## Richard Cuffari

AN
**APPLE**
PAPERBACK

SCHOLASTIC BOOK SERVICES
New York Toronto London Auckland Sydney Tokyo

*For my parents, Sam and Blanche Warren,*
*who provided the chicken bones,*
*and for my brother Buzz who helped me wish*

———————

*Special thanks to Margaret (Bunny) Gabel*
*for her professional expertise and*
*for the warmth of her encouragement.*

———————

ISBN 0-590-31783-0

12 11 10 9 8 7 6 5 4 3 2 1        11        1 2 3 4 5 6/8
Printed in the U.S.A.                        11

# 1

It's NOVEMBER already, but Mr. Magliore, the gym teacher, still takes us outside to play softball. "You fourth graders are too soft. We have to toughen you up," he says.

All the other kids were happy, but I buttoned my sweater all the way to the top. I was shivering so hard when we lined up that I was afraid I'd swallow my baby tooth. I have a real loose one on the bottom.

All Mr. Magliore said was, "Outside with the rest of the class, Joshua."

I wouldn't tell any of the kids, but I wanted to stay in the room. I could practice my times tables. Eight times four is thirty-two. Nine times three is twenty-seven. Six times five is thirty. No matter how many times you say them, they never change. Six times five is always thirty. Not like softball.

I was the last one out the door. The kids were choosing up sides. Mr. Magliore picked Peter Benson and Marjorie Healy to be captains. They had to pick their own teams. "But everybody has to play," Mr. Magliore warned. I think he probably studied to be a judge before he was a gym teacher, because he tries to be so fair.

I don't mind when we count off by two's, "One, two, one, two." Then all the ones go on one team and the two's on the other. But captains! Peter's the strongest hitter but Marjorie's the fastest. She can make it to third base on just a little hit.

I took off my sweater and sat down. Peter won the toss. "I pick Andy."

Marjorie was next. "I pick Scott."

I didn't have to listen until they got to the end of the class. There were lots of clouds. I could see a giraffe with a top hat floating around the sky.

"I pick Annmarie," said Peter.

"I pick Christopher," said Marjorie.

Peter picked his nose while he waited to go again. I could see his sneakers were all scraped away in the toes. He had three knots in his shoelaces. A bandaid was holding one side together. And it's not 'cause he's poor. My brother Benjie's sneakers look like that. He's on the Junior High Soccer Team. I rubbed my sneakers in the dirt to make them look a little older. Maybe I can wear out this pair before I outgrow them.

Everybody was almost picked. The kids on Marjorie's side were yelling, "Pick Sue. We want Sue."

Marjorie never takes orders from anybody. She started to stamp her foot. "I'm the captain. I'll pick whoever I want." She looked at us like we were leftover tomatoes in the supermarket. "And I pick Sue." Her team cheered.

Mr. Magliore blew his whistle. "Let's go. C'mon, Peter, now it's your turn. You kids won't have time to play, you waste so much time choosing."

Good, I hope they take the whole forty minutes. Peter picked. Now it was only me and Mary Lou left. Sometimes it's me and Sue but I saw her give Marjorie a piece of Dubble Bubble before they started to pick.

That giraffe cloud just turned into a giant ship and it's heading for another ship cloud. If they crash into each other it'll rain and we can go into the gym. Mr. Magliore saves games like dodge ball for inside. I don't mind if I get hit out of the circle first because Mr. Magliore has an extra whistle he gives the first one out. It's on a long red and white plastic lanyard. Then you get to run around the outside of the circle and help call out the kids who get hit. He calls you assistant referee.

It was Marjorie's turn. "O.K. I pick Mary Lou."

Boy, I'm going to watch Marjorie extra hard the next time I'm referee. Mr. Magliore blew the whistle. "O.K. Josh, you're on Peter's team. Marjorie's side up at bat first."

I walked to the outfield. That's where all the captains put me. Hardly anybody in the fourth grade can hit out there.

Peter yelled after me, "Hey, Wilson, stand way back. And don't try to catch any fly balls."

The first two innings were slow. I thought about baseball players on TV and I punched my glove to make a good pocket. I spit on it like Peter Benson does. He hardly ever misses a catch. This old glove was my brother's and it must be filled with dried-up spit.

Christopher was up at bat. He's pretty strong, 'cause he's so fat. I moved back even farther so he couldn't reach me. CRACK! A high fly ball. There must be a strong wind. That ball was coming straight to me.

Christopher was running. His team was yelling, "Go, go, run, Joshua will miss it." My team was yelling, too, "Catch it, Josh, catch it." My lunchtime peanut butter and jelly sandwich was up in the back of my throat. I know how to hold my hands up like I'm catching, so I did and prayed for the ball to go away. It was still coming. So I prayed that all the spit would help it stick to the glove.

4

An arm pushed me away.

"I've got it!" It was Andy. He had run over from right field. The peanut butter and jelly slid back into my stomach.

I was up once, in the third inning. The ball hit my bat and popped up. The catcher got it. "Out!" yelled Mr. Magliore. "Time for one more inning." Mr. Magliore clapped his hands. "The score is tied. Let's go, everybody, hustle."

One more inning. I dragged my sneakers in the dirt as I walked to the outfield. I'll bet this was the longest game on record. I wonder if the Board of Education knows how much time Deerfield School kids spend on softball. We should be using our time to advantage, like it says on the report cards.

I punched my glove again. Peter was yelling at us. "Last out. C'mon gang, don't let them get a hit. Tie score, don't let them get a hit. If the score's tied, we can play extra innings."

I didn't want our team to lose, but I sure didn't want to play extra innings.

Marjorie was up at bat. She bites her lower lip. I can tell even from way out in the field. That's how she looks before she wins all the hurdle races. Mr. Magliore calls it determination, but I don't see how making sores on your lip helps you win a game.

The first pitch was a foul tip. Strike one. Good. Just two more to go. The second pitch was another foul behind home plate. How come the catcher only catches those foul balls when I'm up at bat? Strike two. We don't play balls and strikes, just strikes. You have to be in fifth grade to play balls. Otherwise, Mr. Magliore says, we'd really be here all day.

Peter was winding up again. Marjorie hit the ball. Crack! A good one. She was halfway to first. I was supposed to watch the ball, not the runner. It passed the pitcher and short stop. She was on first. The ball bounced off a rock away from the second baseman. Marjorie was on second and the ball was still loose. She was almost to third.

"Get it, Josh, get it!" The kids were yelling to me now. The ball passed the whole infield and was rolling fast right to me. Before I had a chance to get myself nervous I stuck my glove out. The ball bounced into it. I covered it tightly with my right hand. I did it! I couldn't believe it. Mr. Magliore was right. If you stuck your hand out, the glove would catch it.

I caught the hardest darn line drive that was hit today. That was hit in two days. Maybe the hardest that was hit in two weeks. And I still had it right in my glove.

What were the kids yelling about now?

"Throw the ball, dummy, throw the ball," Andy was screaming in my ear. Peter Benson was jumping up and down on the pitcher's mound. I saw Marjorie pass third and start for home.

"Throw the ball. Throw it." My hands were sweating but I threw as hard as I could. The ball went fast and straight. Right to first base. Marjorie crossed home plate. I didn't realize what had happened until Andy threw his hat on the ground and yelled, "Home, you were supposed to throw the ball home, you, you KLUTZ!"

Peter Benson came over. "Wilson, I told you just to stand there and not catch any balls!"

Before I could say anything, Mr. Magliore blew the whistle. "That's it. Everyone line up. It's time to go inside." I looked down at my glove. Only a minute ago, the ball had been there safe in the pocket. Mr. Magliore was calling me. "Let's go, Josh."

I walked slowly so the kids would get into the building ahead of me. I heard some giggles and then Marjorie's voice, "Lucky for us that Joshua Wilson is such a KLUTZ!" Her bottom lip was bleeding.

"Yeah," said Peter. "And we had to get stuck with him."

Mr. Magliore called me again. "Joshua, help me carry some of this stuff inside." I took a catcher's mitt, two bats, and home plate.

"That was a good catch, Josh."

I couldn't answer, I was too busy trying to balance all the equipment. Besides I knew Mr. Magliore was just trying to be nice about my big goof. He had probably studied to be one of those psychologists and a judge before he became a gym teacher.

"Next time, Josh, you watch the runner. If you're not sure, throw the ball to the pitcher."

"Thanks, Mr. Magliore, but I'm not going to be a ball player. I want to be a C.P.A. like my father. That's a certified public accountant." I wasn't sure Mr. Magliore would know, since he spends so much time in gyms.

"I know, Josh. But certified public accountants can play ball too."

I was going to tell him that I never saw a softball glove in my father's office but I tripped when I got to the two steps by the gym entrance. I dropped the catcher's mitt and when I leaned over to pick it up I tripped Mr. Magliore with one of the bats. That made him drop everything he was carrying.

"Gee. I'm sorry, Mr. Magliore."

"That's O.K., Josh."

We picked everything up and Mr. Magliore took one of the bats and home plate away from me. He held the gym door open. "You go first, Josh. I think it's safer that way."

# 2

WHEN I got out of school at 3 o'clock I saw Mom's car. She was honking the horn. "Hey, Josh. Over here!" I ran over to the car quickly. It wasn't raining and only little kids got picked up on sunny days.

Marjorie and some other kids walked by. "Hi, Klutz!" she called out. I tried to lean against the car so the kids wouldn't see my mother. And I hoped that Mom wouldn't hear the kids call me Klutz!

"Josh, your brother has soccer practice after school and I have to go to work. I don't want you home alone. Would you like to go with me?"

I watched the kids chase each other down the street. Some got on the school bus and the ones who lived close like me turned the corner. I got in the car.

Mother had on her white nurse's uniform. On Tuesday afternoons she volunteers at the Hillside Home for the Aged. On her pocket is a little white plastic badge that says: Ruth Wilson, R.N. She can give shots and everything. Mom says she'll go back to work full-time when we're older.

Since Benjie got into seventh grade he's been busy with the soccer team and the basketball team, so she's only got to wait for me to grow older.

It was the first time I'd been inside the nursing home. There was a big round lobby. I could feel my nose scrunching. I have a very sensitive nose. I can tell what's cooking in somebody's house just by passing by. The trouble is smells usually upset my stomach. This smell was causing a double scrunch and my eyes were stinging too. It smelled like they had fish two nights ago and nobody had done the dishes. I sneezed. There was another smell too. Like someone had broken a big bottle of iodine.

Mother saw my nose scrunch. "You're not going to throw up, are you, Josh? That's just a disinfectant, to keep the place free of germs."

No wonder. I could see all the little germs dropping dead from this smell. I just wondered why it didn't kill the people too.

I stayed close to Mother. There were lots of people walking around. Some of the old folks were in wheelchairs. The nurses were in white uniforms. I watched a cart go by loaded with plants and flowers. A girl in a pink-striped uniform was pushing it. She looked like she was in Benjie's class.

"Be careful, Josh." Mother pulled me back by the belt. I had almost walked into the receptionist's desk.

A man came out of an office. Mother introduced him as Dr. Corby, the Director of the Home.

"Well, well," said Dr. Corby. I hate it when grown-ups say well, well. It's because they're trying to think of something nice to say next.

"Isn't this a fine boy! I can see why you are so proud of him, Mrs. Wilson. This is the goalie on the soccer team, I take it."

Mother interrupted quickly. "No, Dr. Corby, that's my older son Benjie. This is Joshua."

"Oh yes, Joshua." Dr. Corby smiled again. "Well, well." He had a lot of teeth that looked as if they were shined and polished every day. "Mrs. Wilson, you go along. Your patients are waiting. I'll find something for Joshua to do."

"Why can't I go with you, Mom?"

"Now Josh, I have to bathe some patients and give them physical therapy. You go with Dr. Corby. He'll find something to keep you busy."

There were lots of doorways down the hall.

Some to the right and some to the left. It was hard to see to the end. I didn't know how I would find Mother again if she disappeared behind one of those doors. And I didn't want to go with this smiling doctor.

"You know, Dr. Corby," Mom said, "Joshua could play the piano in the lounge for some of the patients."

"You play?" Dr. Corby asked me. Now why did Mom tell him? She knows I'm just a beginner and I don't like to play in front of anybody, not even Mr. Wolfe and he's my piano teacher.

Mom blew me a kiss and walked off down the hall. Dr. Corby took my shoulders and steered me into the lounge. My feet were moving forward but I kept turning my head to see which room Mother went into.

CLANG! "Watch it, little boy." It was another rolling cart. This one was filled with medicine and bandages. They were all over the place. This Home could use a traffic cop to direct carts.

"Well, well. This is Joshua, everybody." Dr. Corby's smile was a fake. I could tell, 'cause it never moved. Like his plastic nametag that said, Dr. Corby, Dir. That means Director.

He kept talking to the room. "This is Joshua. He's going to play the piano for you." He patted my shoulder and left.

There were three old ladies sitting in big

stuffed armchairs in a corner. Another lady was nearby, but she was in a wheelchair with a blanket over her knees. I could feel the scrunching again. That strong germ killer was in this room. There were some hanging plants in front of the window. They looked brown and scraggly. The nurses must scrub them with that smelly stuff too.

Two old men were working on a picture puzzle. I was surprised. I thought just kids liked puzzles. Some others were watching a western on TV. They were sitting real close to the set and it was blasting into the room. If my mother walked in, she would tell them it wasn't good to sit so close to the TV.

An old lady walked up to me. "You look like my grandson," she said. She took a picture out of her pocket. You're not supposed to stare at people but she was so old. She was tiny and stooped over, just a little bit taller than I am. And she was covered with wrinkles. They started at the top of her head and went all the way down her neck and covered her hands. She was squashed together like an accordion.

She didn't look like my grandmother at all. My grandmother has blonde hair and she wears high-heeled shoes and dances the cha cha with Grandpa in Miami Beach.

I started to count the wrinkles in the old lady's face.

"I'm Mrs. Horowitz," said a big wrinkle that

turned out to be her mouth. "Please play something for us. My grandson can play the piano too." I tried to look at the picture of her grandson but she put it back in her pocket.

"Yes," said one of the men from the picture puzzle. "Can you play the song *Rumania?*" Mrs. Horowitz walked me over to the piano. She smelled nice, like peppermint Life Savers. I sat down.

The lady in the wheelchair called me. "Can you play *My Wild Irish Rose?*"

The piano was an old upright. The bench was too high. My feet couldn't touch the floor. Some of the piano keys were yellow and peeling.

"Can you play *Golden Earrings?*" asked one of the old men near the TV set.

Mrs. Horowitz smiled. "My grandson knows *Tie a Yellow Ribbon Round the Old Oak Tree.* I'll bet you know it too."

I know the top twenty-five hits of the day, because Benjie always plays WABC on the radio. But I never heard of these songs, except for *Tie a Yellow Ribbon.* And I can't play it on the piano. I mostly do just scales and exercises. The only whole song I know by heart is *The Spinning Song.*

It's only three lines, but you play them twice each. I have trouble with the last chord because my fingers can't stretch a whole octave from C to C. My pinky just gives up when it reaches A.

14

Maybe if I told them I was a pitcher and my arms were tired from throwing the ball all day, I wouldn't have to play. I don't think they know any fourth graders from Deerfield.

CRACK! I heard a whip. My knees bumped the piano as I turned to the doorway.

It wasn't a whip. And I forgot to rub my knees. Standing there was a giant man who was cracking a riding stick against the wall.

CRACK! "Vell, Mrs. Horovitz." CRACK! "Vell. Who ve have here?" asked the giant. He stopped cracking the stick but he pointed it right at me!

# 3

IF MRS. HOROWITZ was squashed in half, this man was stretched almost to the ceiling. He didn't have any slump in his body. I'll bet no one ever had to tell him to stand up straight the way Mom tells me. He had all this hair down to his shoulders and a beard that started under his nose with a big mustache and grew all the way down his chest. Maybe he was a hippie? But all the hair was white. Even his eyebrows. They were real bushy and grew over his nose. He had so much hair, I couldn't tell how old he was.

The man cleared his throat. "AAAAAAAAA-AAAHHHHHHHHHHHHHHHEEEEEEEEEEEEEEE-MMMMMMMMMMMMMM! You are finished staring, Joshua?"

I forgot I was sitting at a piano and my elbows banged down on the piano keys. The man stared back at me. He had a funny shirt. It was reddish and buttoned on the side by his neck instead of in front. It didn't have a collar or a tie, just stood up straight around his face. It had these big sleeves and he had a ribbon around his waist instead of a belt. His pants were dark and they were tucked into high shiny black leather boots. And he kept slapping the boots with that big riding stick. I don't know anyplace you can go horseback riding around Millburn.

"Mrs. Horovitz. Back to chair. I take over now." He tapped Mrs. Horowitz on the shoulder with the stick, but real light. He didn't hurt her.

"Oh dear, just when the boy was going to play for us."

"Please, Mrs. Horovitz. He play ven I tell him."

It wasn't only his clothes that were funny. His words were too. He didn't sound like he was talking American. His w's were all mixed up with his v's, like a spy on one of those mystery TV shows.

He came closer to the piano and I saw that he wasn't a giant, just that he stood so straight. As if he were at attention in a parade. "Vell, Joshua— now you *play!*" He made it sound like an order, the same way Mr. Magliore sounds when he says, "Class—line up!"

"How did you know I'm Joshua?" I asked.

He tapped me on the head with the riding crop. Tap. Tap. "Because I *know*," was his answer. "Vell, Joshua, vat you going to play?"

I didn't answer and I guess my mouth must have been open because he said, "Please close mouth, Joshua. Vhen I vas on maneuvers vith my troops, ve once lost cavalryman because he kept mouth open and bee flew in."

I swallowed. "What happened to him?"

"Vat happened you ask? Vat happened?" The man drew himself up straighter and pulled at his beard. "The bee flew down soldier's gullet into his stomach and opened vings and began to fly. Zoom, into the liver. ZZZZZOOOOOOOMMMMMM-MMMMMM into the intestines, ZZZZZZZOO-OOOOOOMMMMMMMMMMMM into the gall bladder. Looking for vay out of stomach."

I made my mouth real small and asked, "Did he get out?"

The man pulled over a chair. He sat but his shoulders stayed as straight as if he were standing. "Ve never found out. The bee became so angry that zzzzzzzzzoooooooooommmmmmmmmm, bbbb-bbbbbbuuuuuuuuuuuzzzzzzzzzz, ssssssssssttttttttt-iiiiiiiiiinnnnnnnnnngggggggggg! He stung cavalry-man right on appendix."

I almost fell off the bench. "On the appendix?"

"That is right. Cavalryman vas so surprised he jumped in saddle and his spurs kicked horse and horse reared up, jumped over hedge, leaped across brook, and galloped off to China. Ve never saw either of them again." CRACK! The stick came down on top of the piano. "Now play."

I started *The Spinning Song.* I played it straight through. When I finished the old folks were clapping. They were clapping for me. The man tapped me on the head again and boomed out, *"Ochin Khorosho!"*

I couldn't figure out what that meant, and I guess he could tell, because he said, "That means very good. I forget Americans only know own words. Now play more."

"I only know *The Spinning Song.*"

"Very vell," said the man. "Play it again."

I did. I played it through three times. And the last time my pinky even reached the C and I played a perfect chord.

"That is very nice *Spinning Song,* Joshua. Next time, another song you learn."

His voice made me sit straighter and I tried to push back my shoulders the way he did. "Thank you. But it took me six weeks to learn this song. I can't learn another one so quick."

The stick slammed down on the piano top. This time it wasn't light. It shook the bench. *"Nyet!* No soldier of mine ever say, I can't." BAM! The stick hit the piano top again. The piano keys were shaking.

"Take off shoes."

"What?" I said.

"Shoes. Take off, and the socks. Come, come quickly. Shoes and socks off."

I looked around, but nobody was paying attention. I took off my sneakers and looked up at the man. The stick crashed down on the piano again. I took off my socks.

"Now," he said, "count toes."

"Count my toes?"

He snorted through his nose like he was getting mad at me. "You know how to follow orders?"

I nodded and stuck my chest out. "Yes!"

"*Ochin Khorosho*. So count toes."

I counted. "One, two three . . ." This was silly. I almost giggled. I was sitting in a room with a bunch of old people with my shoes and socks off counting toes. "Four, five." I couldn't hold back the giggles, but I coughed a few times to hide them.

"There." I sat up. "I counted them. I have ten toes."

"You are sure?" The man tapped the floor with his stick.

For a minute I was worried. I looked down at my feet again and wiggled my toes. No, there they were, all ten of them. I stared right back. "Yes, I have ten. Five on each foot."

He reached out and put a hand across my eyes.

"You are sure. Now tell me. How many toes you have?"

I could feel my heart thump. I couldn't see through his fingers, they were so tight across my eyes. But I wasn't going to change my mind. I knew I had ten toes. And so right out loud I said, "Ten. I'm sure. I have ten toes."

The man took his hands down. "*Ochin Khorosho*. Now I show you something." He started to pull his own boots off but then told me to help him. I grabbed hold of the heel and pulled. One boot off. Then the other and finally the socks. The man sat back. "Count toes."

I counted. The right foot. "One, two, three, four . . ." I stopped and counted again. "One, two, three, four . . ." There were only four toes on the right foot. I looked at the left foot. "One, two, three, four, five, SIX!" Six toes! The left foot had six toes. Ten toes altogether but four on one foot and six on the other. I scratched my head.

The man tapped his right foot. "It happened on march in Siberia. Many, many years ago. So cold it vas. BBBBBBBBBRRRRRRRRRRRR . . . Ice and snow, snow and ice all around. Ve forced to valk. Couldn't ride horses. Snow vas too deep. Up to hips." He stood up and showed me on his leg how high the snow came up.

"Right through boots. Toes got colder and colder and bluer and bluer, 'till I could not feel

21

them anymore. Doctor said, 'FROSTBITE!' Doctor took my saber and WHAP . . . cut off little toe."
The man cracked his riding stick on the ground. I had the shivers and I looked down at my own feet. But there they were, all my ten toes, pink and wiggling.

The man pointed to his left foot. "I took out magic chicken vishbone and vished and vished and vished for toe grow back again."

"A magic chicken bone?" I asked. "What happened?"

"Vell, I guess Siberia too cold for vishes to come through right. I think my vish got frostbite and all mixed up." The man sighed. "I grew back toe but on wrong foot. That's how I got six toes on my left."

I forgot and banged the piano with my elbows again. "What were you doing in Siberia?"

The man drew himself up straight. Even with his boots off, his back was stiff and his six on one side, four on the other side toes were flat on the ground. They didn't even wiggle. "Vat I vas doing in Siberia? You don't know me?"

I looked real close again. No, I would have remembered if I'd met him before or if he was on TV. "No, I don't know you."

He fluffed his hair and his white beard with his fingers. Then he sort of smoothed down the front

of his blouse and said, "I am Nicolai, Ivanovitch, Petrov, Romanoff, the Czar of Russia."

"The Czar of Russia!" It's lucky that there were no bees in the old age home, because I forgot to keep my mouth closed and I probably would have swallowed a dozen.

Then the man sat down and put his hands in his pockets. "Vell, I'm really Czar of Markovo, vich is small suburb inside Siberia. Vich I lost toe trying to find. But if it hadn't been for chicken vishbone, I vould be Czar of Russia!"

# 4

As SOON as I got home, I ran to look for Benjie's world globe. We sleep in the same room. It's all red, white, and blue and has pictures of ships on the walls. Mother decorated it. She found two round life preservers in an old shipyard. Dad painted "Benjie" on one in blue and "Joshua" on one in red. They're supposed to hang over our beds for headboards. Only Benjie took his down when he got into seventh grade and hung up a poster of Joe Namath. He also took down most of the ship pictures and hung up the Miami Dolphins and some basketball players. I thought Mom would feel bad 'cause she spent so much time fixing it up, but all she said was, "Don't make holes in the walls, Benjie."

I found the globe on the top shelf of the closet. I had to blow the dust off. I spun it around until I found the U.S.S.R. That's what they call Russia on maps. I got real excited when I found Siberia. If only I could find Markovo.

Benjie walked in. He was just coming back from soccer practice and he had on his blue warm-up suit. He saw me with the globe. "I told you not to touch anything on my side of the room."

"But Benjie, this wasn't on your side. It was in the closet."

"It was on my side of the closet. And it's my globe. PUT IT BACK, before I rearrange your face!"

"I just want to find a city in Siberia. And you don't even use it."

"Doesn't matter. It's mine." He came over to me. "What are you looking for?"

"Markovo."

"Never heard of it." Sometimes Benjie thinks he knows everything. Just because he's in junior high.

He leaned over the globe and shoved me away. "I see Moscow," he said.

"No, the name is Markovo, and it's in Siberia."

"Here's a city named Magodan."

"Nope."

"Murmansk?"

"No. I told you it's in Siberia!"

"Ah, I bet there's no such place." Benjie gave

the globe a smack and it went spinning around. All the countries and oceans blurred together. "And besides, I told you not to touch my stuff. Now put it back!" I knew that was an order. I'd have to ask the Czar exactly where Markovo was.

Mom called us into dinner. Dad was tossing the salad. He can flip tomatoes and cucumbers and radishes in mid-air. He does pancakes too. Mother says it's because his wrists are double-jointed. Benjie tosses a basketball like that. He says he's double-jointed in the wrists too.

Dad had on his green warm-up suit. It has the same white stripe down the side that Benjie's has. Every Tuesday night, Dad plays at the indoor tennis courts in town. I have a warm-up suit too. It's blue, like Benjie's. I just haven't found any sport I want to warm-up for.

You have to be fast in this family if you want to talk at dinner. Benjie was chewing carrot sticks and telling about his soccer practice. We had to hear how he blocked every single goal. His side won 7–3. I wanted to ask how come the other team scored three points if he blocked every goal, but Dad started talking about his new tennis racket. It has this big head and it's going to improve his serve.

Mother interrupted. "Benjie, you hid your peas under your plate and Josh, you have dust on your nose. Didn't you wash before dinner?"

Benjie had to put the peas back on his plate so I had a chance to talk. "I met a Czar today." That got 'em! They stopped chewing and looked at me. So I told about the Home, *The Spinning Song*, and about the Czar.

Mother smiled. "I've met your Czar at the Home a few times. He's quite a character."

Benjie had put the peas back on his plate and now he was trying to mash them under his potatoes. "That's why you were trying to find that place in Siberia. It's not on the map. The guy must be a fake."

"He is not a fake." I pushed my plate away.

"Boys, stop it." Mother pushed my plate back. "Actually no one knows where Mr. Romanoff comes from. They found him sitting outside the Home one morning waiting for it to open."

"Doesn't he have a family?" asked Dad.

"No one knows," Mother said. "Dr. Corby told him the Home was full, but he just sat there all day and when it got dark they took him inside and gave him a room. And he's been there ever since."

"Does he have any money?" asked Benjie.

"Yes, as a matter of fact he has a bank account and he says he has an army pension. He gives the Home a check every month for his room and board."

"See," I said. "He's not a fake. That's probably

from the Russian army. I made a deal to visit him every Tuesday."

"That's nice, Josh. You'll go with me." Mom pointed to Benjie's plate. "I see those peas you're trying to hide under the potatoes."

The phone rang. "For you, Josh," said Dad. At first all I heard were some giggles. I thought it was one of those phony phone calls where the people hang up without saying anything. A squeaky voice said, "Is this Joshua Wilson?" More giggles. I had finished eating, but my stomach was making a warning growl. The voice screamed out, "HEY, JOSHUA WILSON, YOU ARE A KLUTZ!" Slam went the receiver and all that was left was the buzzing phone.

"Don't you want dessert, Josh?" Mother asked me.

"No thanks." I didn't feel so good. I went to my room to lie down. I couldn't even keep my shoulders straight like the Czar's anymore today. My ears were hurting from that word, Klutz. I tried to figure out who called. Andy? Marjorie? It could be any kid in the class.

Benjie came in and turned on the light. He lay down in front of our closet-door mirror and put on his ankle weights. He was going to do his leg exercises. "One, two, three, four . . . Hey, Joshua, what's the matter?"

I sat up and leaned over the bed to watch. I counted with him. ". . . Seven, eight, nine . . . Do you think if I used your weights they'd help me run faster?"

Benjie looked me over. "You're in pretty bad shape, but I guess you have to start somewhere."

I got down on the floor and he tied the weights on my ankles. "We'll start you with two pounds on each leg," he said. "Now, remember, you've got to keep your knees straight when you lift your legs." When Benjie acted like a person, which wasn't often, it wasn't too bad to be his brother. I told him about the softball game and the telephone call. "Benjie, do you think I should tell Mr. Magliore that the kids are calling me Klutz?"

Benjie was tying knots in the weights. "Don't be stupid. You remember my friend, Gary?"

I nodded.

"Well, once when we were in third or fourth grade we were coming back from a field trip to New York City. Just as we got near the Lincoln Tunnel, Gary puked. I mean he barfed all over the bus."

While Benjie was talking I tried to lift my right leg and my left went up in the air at the same time. Benjie had to sit on it to keep it down. He continued, "By the time we got back to school everyone was calling Gary Vomit-head."

"Vomit-head?" My right foot banged the floor.

Benjie switched and sat on my right leg so I could lift the left one.

"Yeah, and from that day on we teased him and called him Vomit-head."

"What happened?"

"Well, Gary's mother came to school and she was really mad. She talked to the principal and the teachers and they gave us a big lecture about how mean we were and how Gary was crying and didn't want to come to school and how we shouldn't call names."

"Did you stop calling him Vomit-head?"

"Not exactly. When we saw him we'd yell here comes TSVH!"

"TSVH. What did that mean?"

"Here comes The Squealing Vomit-Head!"

I thought about it. "I guess I better not tell." I could just hear Marjorie calling me The Squealing Klutz.

"I guess not. Now come on. Move those legs."

I tried. My stomach hurt from trying to raise my legs and keep them straight at the same time. Benjie said that was good. The leg exercises would toughen my guts!

Benjie rolled off my right leg. "Now, both legs up in the air." I put them up. "Now hold them straight and together, while I count to ten. One, two, three . . ." You wouldn't think ten was such a long time to hold legs in the air. But it felt like

31

ten times a hundred, 'cause he counted so slow. "Four, five . . ." I couldn't hold them up anymore. Crash! The weights pulled them to the ground. My right leg caught the cord from Benjie's lamp and it tipped over.

"The lamp," hollered Benjie. I tried to get up too quickly and banged my head on the edge of the desk chair. The lamp hit the floor. I picked it up and gave it to Benjie. I rubbed my head. My eyes were stinging and I could feel a bump starting to grow.

"It didn't break," I said. Benjie replugged the lamp and straightened up the desk top.

"Take off my ankle weights!" he yelled.

I tried to undo them. He had tied the knots too tight.

"You're tangling the laces!" He pushed my fingers away and started to untie. "You really are! You know that? You really are!"

"Are what, Benjie?"

"A KLUTZ, Joshua Wilson. A Grade A—KLUTZ!"

# 5

"Everybody up. Hurry. Benjie, you'll miss the bus!" Mother woke us the same way every morning. Benjie grunted and put the pillow over his head. I started to get out of bed. ow! Something was wrong with my legs. Everytime I moved I felt iron clamps on the back. I slid my whole body over to the edge and pushed my legs over the side. ow! Maybe I had caught some disease overnight. Benjie always kept the window open. Once in current events, someone had brought in an article that told about a kid getting a disease from his pet parrot. Anything could fly in our open window!

I stood up. The only way I could walk was stiff-legged. My knees wouldn't bend. I felt like a wind-up toy soldier. "Hey, Benjie." I shook him. "Wake up. I'm crippled. You better call Mom."

"How'd you like your teeth rearranged? I'll save Dad money on braces." He curled up tighter in the corner.

I was too worried about the disease in my legs to care about getting him mad. I shook him again. ow! When my legs shook that pain went up and down the backs. "Benjie. I'm not kidding. Something's wrong with my legs."

He sat up and threw the pillow at me. His double-joints don't work so good in the morning. He missed. But he reached down and grabbed the back of my legs and massaged them up and down like they were cookie dough. "It's nothing. Just sore muscles from lifting weights last night."

"Oh." I had forgotten about the weights. Here I thought there'd be a big telethon about me and all the movie stars would come on to raise money for my unknown disease. They might even have put me on posters. But I don't think Benjie would take Joe Namath down to put me up, he's too mean.

"I guess I better not lift weights anymore."

Benjie jumped out of bed. "Don't be stupid. You've got to. Every night. Otherwise your legs will just hurt all over again."

Mother was calling. I tried to hurry, but it hurt when I moved too fast. I put on my sneakers and thought of the Czar. I'll bet he hadn't complained when the doctor zapped his toe off! He had just wrapped his foot in a handkerchief and shoved it back in the boot. So I guess I could stand a little pins and needles in my legs.

Mom was pouring orange juice. I walked to the window and looked at the thermometer that was stuck in the flower box. "It's 65 degrees. Don't you think that's too cold to play outside?"

She laughed. "Of course not. It's clear and lovely, just right."

I found a pit in the bottom of my orange juice. I tried to drink while holding the pit away with my tongue. "Do you think it'll rain today?"

"I hope not. I've got lots of things to do. Besides, pretty soon, the weather will get cold and we'll all be wishing for these nice days."

I wouldn't. I remembered that phone call last night. I wished it was as cold as Siberia and piled up with snow. Then for sure we wouldn't have to play softball. Because as long as we have to play, everybody will remember what a klutz I am. I got my books from the counter.

"Josh," Mom asked, "why are you walking so funny? What's the matter with your legs?"

I started to get hopeful again. "I was doing exercises with Benjie last night. Maybe I shouldn't go to school today?"

"No, you go to school. The legs will only get stiffer if you lie around the house."

"But maybe you could write a note, so I wouldn't have to take gym?"

"Now, Josh." Mother zipped up my windbreaker. "Gym will be good for your legs. You'll take a nice hot bath tonight and all the aches will be gone."

I thought of that giggling telephone voice. My throat felt tight. "Mother, I think my throat hurts a little . . ."

She put her hand on my forehead and cheek. "You're fine, Josh, now off to school."

I don't care if she is a registered nurse. "Don't you think you should use a thermometer?" I asked.

"Josh." Mother had her no-more-fooling-around-voice. "There's nothing wrong with you. Why are you looking for an excuse to stay home?"

"See you later, Mom." Benjie ran through the kitchen grabbing his books from the counter.

"Benjie, you didn't drink your juice," yelled Mother.

I followed him out the open door.

The bell hadn't rung yet. There were lots of kids around Marjorie's desk. I was listening for that giggle, but Marjorie just said, "Hi, Josh."

I sat down. I had to stretch my legs way out in front so they wouldn't bend. All the kids were busy with something. I took out my colored pencils and a piece of drawing paper. I closed my eyes

36

and tried to imagine what Siberia looked like.
Then I drew big mounds of snow and large trees
without any leaves on them. I had to use my gray
pencil for the snow because white didn't show up
on white paper. The gray made it sort of dirty
looking, like city snow. I started to draw some soldiers marching in the snow.

Miss Garett called the class to order. I thought
red uniforms would look nice. Miss Garett called
for reading workbooks. I'd have time to finish before she got to me. I drew swords, just like the one
the doctor used to zap off the Czar's toe. Maybe if
the picture came out good enough I could mail it to
the Czar.

Mr. Magliore popped his head in the door. "I
just wanted to say good morning. I'll see all you
great softball players fourth period." Miss Garett
walked over to the door to talk to him.

Marjorie put her hands around her mouth like a
large funnel. "He loves her." The kids giggled. I
looked up at the door. Sure enough Miss Garett's
face was all pink. Marjorie's whisper was louder.
"I heard Mr. Magliore's going to marry her." She
fell over her desk laughing and Sue had to smack
her on the back.

I took a black pencil to make the shiny leather
boots. If I were Mr. Magliore and had his muscles
and could hit a ball over the third base fence, I
wouldn't bother with any girls.

Uh oh. Miss Garett was back to business. "Workbooks please, class." And she tapped her desk with the ruler. Maybe I should name my picture like they do in the museums. I could call it, "Looking for Markovo."

"Joshua, I don't see your workbook." I pushed the picture to the side of my desk. I'd finish it later. I had to walk to the back of the room to get my reading workbook. I was still walking pretty stiff because of my legs and when I passed Marjorie's desk I tripped over something. As I fell I saw her metal lunch box right in the middle of the aisle. I hit against the game table and a box of chinese checkers tipped over. All the marbles spilled out and hit the floor with a clatter. I bent down and tried to stop them from rolling all over the room. The kids started to laugh and they got on the floor to catch rolling marbles.

Miss Garett pounded her desk for quiet. Peter Benson caught a couple of purples and shot them to me. "Here, KLUTZ, catch!" They went past me to Marjorie. She caught them and shot them back to Peter. Miss Garett was yelling. "This class had better come to order. Joshua Wilson, get up. Peter Benson, get in your seat. Marjorie, turn around and face front. Joshua, I'm not going to speak to you again!"

"But Miss Garett . . ." I had picked up about

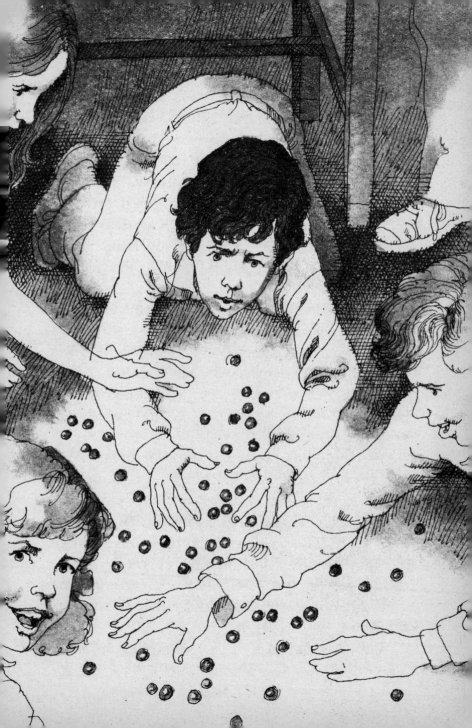

eight marbles. I was trying to put them back in the game.

"Joshua, sit down right now!" Miss Garett's voice ended in a scream. I hurried back to my seat and tripped over that lunch box again. The whole class was hysterical laughing.

"This class will come to order." Miss Garett's face was beet red. "Now Joshua, suppose you stay after school with me this afternoon and explain just why you can't walk up and down an aisle without tripping."

"But Miss Garett . . ." I started to point to Marjorie's lunch box in the middle of the aisle. It wasn't there. All of a sudden, the class was real quiet. I wiped my hands on my pants.

Marjorie had her hands folded and she was studying the ceiling as if the whole alphabet of the world was printed on it. The middle of my stomach felt cold. None of the kids were looking at me. They were all like Marjorie, looking at the ceiling or straight ahead.

I remembered the story Benjie told me last night. I better not squeal about the lunch box. I didn't want the kids to call me a klutz *and* a fink.

Miss Garett was pushing papers around her desk. "And as for the rest of the class, you will all be punished for causing such an uproar." Miss Garett stopped for a minute. Everybody held his breath. I could tell she was trying to think up something terrible. "No gym!" The kids moaned. "There will be no gym this morning. You'll stay in the room and write a composition on Good Manners in the Classroom!"

She started to put problems on the blackboard. There was a loud whisper from the back. "This is all because of you, you klutz!"

My face was hot and sticky and it wasn't just from tripping. And my throat was really starting to hurt. The picture had fallen off my desk and when I picked it up there was a big dirty footprint on it. "Klutz!" I knew that was Marjorie. Why was everybody blaming me because we weren't going to gym? I tried to brush the dirt off the picture. Well, I still had almost a week before I saw the Czar. I could draw it over again. Right now, I just wished I could jump into one of those big snow piles and disappear.

# 6

MISS GARETT·let me off pretty easy. She just said how surprised she was that a good student like me would clown around to get attention. "You should be an example to the other students, Joshua." I guess she doesn't know our class too well if she thinks anybody would want to copy me!

The weather was nice all week, but we had to take achievement tests so we missed more gym. I must have been the only happy one, 'cause the rest of the kids moaned and groaned. Mr. Magliore stopped in every morning to say hello to us. For once I think Marjorie must be right, because Miss Garett gets all red when he comes in and I don't think he can like fourth graders that much. He promised us a double gym session when we got through with our tests.

My legs finally stopped hurting, but Benjie started me working on my arm muscles and my shoulders hurt even when I moved a pencil.

Friday morning Miss Garett gave us ten minutes to study spelling before our weekly word test. We had to study with the person across the aisle from us. Christopher and I pushed our desks together.

Christopher just moved here in September. He's twice as big as any of the other kids, but he has lots of friends. I've been in this school since kindergarten and I still don't get invited to play after school unless it's a birthday party that the whole class goes to.

Christopher wears striped polo shirts, the ones that have those alligators crawling around. I wear them too. His shirts never stay tucked in. He always has some belly sticking out.

When he first came, Peter Benson called him "Jelly Belly." All the kids picked it up. "Jelly Belly. Jelly Belly." So one day in the playground, Christopher tackled Peter Benson and sat on him. "Who're you calling Jelly Belly?" he asked. Then he bounced up and down on Peter's belly until Peter yelled, "Stop!"

I never heard anybody call Christopher "Jelly Belly" again. At least not out loud. And he still has a big white roll of stomach that sticks out.

We took turns testing each other. Christopher

was almost as good as I am. He got stuck on apostrophes. "I don't think apostrophes should count," he said. "They're not letters. Why should I get a whole word wrong because of one little black mark?"

I tried to explain apostrophes. Christopher said, "O.K., if you're so smart, how do you remember where to put them?"

"Maybe this sounds crazy," I said, "but I think I've got a photographic memory and in the middle of a test, I just close my eyes, use my photographic memory, and WHAM, I remember how the word looked and write it on the paper."

Christopher was chewing on the end of his pencil. "So how come you can't use that photographic memory when you play ball?"

Marjorie stopped in front of us. "Hey, move your desks, I can't get by."

"Take the subway!" said Christopher. He and Marjorie stared at each other 'til she finally shook her head and walked around our desks saying, "Oh I wouldn't want to disturb the KLUTZ anyway. He'll fall out of his desk and we'll lose some more gym periods."

Christopher pointed the chewed-up end of his pencil at me. "You ought to slug her, Wilson. I'll sit on her at lunchtime if you want."

It was time for the test. Christopher and I marked each other's papers and we both got 100 percent. Miss Garett went up to the spelling chart that was pinned to the bulletin board. She said, "Joshua Wilson got moved up to SUPER POWER today and Christopher is in AIRBORNE."

The lowest group was called COUNT DOWN. Miss Garett thought of funny names for our subjects. All the teachers did. It was supposed to fool the slow kids so they wouldn't feel bad about not being in the fastest group. I watched her color in purple for SUPER POWER. Marjorie was still in BLAST OFF. I looked across at her, hoping she'd see my purple column, but she had her head stuck in a book and never looked up at the blackboard. I checked, but her lunch box was under her desk where it was supposed to be.

At lunch, Christopher and I were the last ones left at the table. The other kids gulp down their sandwiches so they can go outside and shoot baskets. Christopher eats fast too. It's just that he has twice as much lunch to eat as everyone else.

"Hey, Wilson, how come you chew so slow?" Christopher was watching me eat.

"It's not healthy to eat too fast." I didn't want to tell him that if I ate too fast, there'd be too much time left to go outside and then I'd have to shoot baskets.

Christopher kept eating. He had asked me something, I guess I could ask him back. "Is that a tuna fish sandwich?"

"Yeah!"

"Does your mother make tuna fish with celery or lettuce?"

Christopher lifted a corner of the bread. "Both."

"Oh." I looked at my own sandwich and told Christopher, "My mother makes mine with lettuce. My dad and brother like celery. I don't. You want to know why?"

"Yeah, I can't wait." Christopher took a big bite. Some of the tuna fish squirted out of the sides of his sandwich. "Why?"

"Strings."

"Strings?" Christopher stopped chewing.

"Yeah. Celery has all those stringy strings when you chew it. They get caught in my teeth and make me gag."

Christopher opened his sandwich and started to pick out the pieces of celery that were in his tuna fish.

I finished mine. Mom cuts the crusts off my bread, but I still leave pieces where I think the crust would be.

Christopher bit into an apple. I pointed to it. "You know, Christopher, I know how to save you if you start to choke on that apple."

He rolled up his paper lunch bag. "Yeah, how?"

"See, my mother is a nurse. She's always teaching me first aid. Say you swallowed a big piece of apple. It could get caught in your throat and you wouldn't be able to breathe."

"So?" When Christopher stopped chewing, I knew he was listening.

"Well, everybody would think you were having a heart attack. But you're supposed to grab the person around the waist and punch him hard and that'll make him spit up the food he's choking on."

Christopher stood up. "Show me."

I got up. "Turn around, Christopher. Make believe you're choking."

Christopher started stamping his feet and coughing and throwing his head around. I tried to grab him around the waist. "Hold still, Christopher." But he was having too much fun. He was snorting and jogging up and down like a wild pony, not like somebody who was choking.

"Christopher, if you were choking you wouldn't be able to move so fast. Hold still so I can save you!"

He put his hands up to his throat and started to go, "Gagagaga gagagagag . . ." I tried to punch him in the waist. Once. I tried again. My fist just got buried in his belly roll that felt like a rubber pillow.

"Am I saved yet?"

I tried again. I was getting out of breath from trying to hold Christopher tight around the middle and punch him at the same time. My fist hit something sharp. His belt buckle. His polo was way up around his stomach and the alligator was crawling around his shoulder.

"Boy. That's a sharp belt buckle you got." I shook my wrist. "Let me see it."

"Ah, it's nothing." He tried to pull his shirt over his pants. But I saw the big square metal buckle with the picture on it.

"Hey, Christopher, look." I lifted up my sweater and showed him the same Captain Future, Space 3000 buckle. "We could be twins." I couldn't think of anybody else in the fourth grade who had one.

Christopher touched my buckle. "Did you send away for yours from the station or the magazine? You watch after school or on Saturdays?"

I watched *Captain Future, Space 3000* every day after school. Unless Mother turns off the TV and makes me go out for fresh air.

Christopher kept asking questions. "Do you collect all the magazines? My father got me a subscription. But I'm missing some. I'll trade with you if you want."

I get the magazine too. Grandma gave me a subscription for my birthday. Benjie thought it was dumb. He gets *Sports Magazine*. But I like *Space 3000*. They tell you what everything's going to be like in the future. Captain Future has adventures with strange planets and space people. And they don't play games like we do. In the future they just put this paper in the computer with the teams' names on it. The computer plays the whole game and tells you who won.

"I'll trade with you, Christopher. Do you have pictures of the whole space crew?"

"Most of them. Some aren't too good. Listen, you want to come over to my house this afternoon?"

Boy, it was lucky I had worn my space buckle today. "Sure."

"O.K. You go home first and get your magazines and then come over and we'll trade."

"O.K."

There was a tap on the window. Peter Benson and Andy were shooting baskets and calling for Christopher. "I'm going out now. You want to come?"

"No, I don't feel like it. I'll see you after school."

He crumpled his milk carton and tossed it into the garbage can. There was half a cookie left in his wax paper. He popped it into his mouth and headed for the door.

"Hey, Christopher, I don't know where your house is."

"747 Sunset. Right around the corner from Peter's."

I didn't know where Peter's house was, but Sunset wasn't far. I could find it.

"747 Sunset." I cleaned up my own crumbs and crumpled my milk carton the same way Christopher had. Then I aimed a onehander at the garbage can. The milk carton made a big curve and dropped right in.

"Hey, did you see that? Right in on the first try." I looked all around, but nobody was left in the lunch room except Mr. Duncan the janitor and he was way down at the other end.

# 7

I RAN straight home after school. "Can't stop for a snack, Mom. I'm going over to my friend Christopher's house." Well, maybe he wasn't my real friend yet, but he did invite me to play.

I dug out a stack of *Space 3000* magazines. Mother followed me into my room. "Where are you going with those, Josh?"

"Me and Christopher are going to trade."

I dug around the bottom of the closet and found the canvas carrier bag that Benjie used when he was a paper boy. It was on his side of the closet, but he wouldn't miss it. He had only been a paper boy for three weeks. It had rained every day, four people went on vacation and wouldn't pay, and Mom said she wasn't going to get up 6 o'clock in the morning to drive him around.

Before I left, I asked Mom, "Did you mail that picture to the Czar? The one I gave you the other day?"

"No, Josh. I didn't mail it." She held up her hand as I started to make a face. "But I dropped it off when I was shopping. Dr. Corby promised to give it to Mr. Romanoff."

I wish she had mailed it. Old smiley Dr. Corby would probably make the nurses spray it with germ killer before he let the Czar have it.

I passed Peter Benson's house before I got to Sunset Street. I knew it was his house 'cause he and Andy were tossing a ball. "Hey, Klutz," yelled Peter, "where you going?" Too bad I couldn't sit on him!

"I'm going to Christopher's."

"What do you have in that bag, Wilson? Don't tell me you're a paper boy?" Andy slapped my canvas bag. "Boy, the people you deliver to probably find their papers in the sewer." They started tossing the ball again, but I could still hear them laughing as I walked down the street.

I turned the corner, 742, 745, there it was, 747. I pushed the bag to my other shoulder and rang the bell.

Christopher answered. He was chewing a long pretzel stick. "Hi," he said between chews. "You brought the books? Neat!" He dumped the magazines right in the middle of the living room floor.

"I have this one about the Alpha Colony. Hey, this is when Captain Future meets the invaders from Septernia. I don't have that one." He had another pretzel stuck in his back pocket. "Do you want a snack? We got time before the show starts. Come into the kitchen."

Christopher took out chocolate cupcakes and pound cake and chocolate chip cookies. He poured two tall glasses of milk and stirred in chocolate syrup.

I looked around the kitchen. His mother had hanging plants over the window and little notes pinned to the bulletin board just like at my house.

A door slammed and a girl walked into the kitchen. She looked just like Christopher except she had long blonde hair and his is short.

"This is my sister Cindy," mumbled Christopher.

She tried to put her arms around him. "Oh my little baby brother brought a friend home to play."

"Stop that!" He pushed her away.

The door opened and another blonde girl walked in. Christopher didn't even look up. "That's Carol, my other sister. They're twins."

"Well, well," she said, "looks like Christopher was first one home and first one at the refrigerator."

Both girls were as fat as Christopher but their sweaters were tucked in. I didn't see any belly rolls hanging out on them.

Christopher drank his milk. The girls were singing—two different songs.

"Now you see why I don't like to bring friends home."

"I heard that," said Cindy as she tapped him on his head. I could tell which was which because they had their names written in red thread on the collars of their blouses.

Carol joined in. "You know, sweet brother, we're supposed to take charge of you when Mother's not home."

"Yeah, but you're not supposed to bother me when I have friends over."

Carol made a fist. "Bother you! Listen, baby brother, how would you like a fat lip to match your fat stomach?"

Christopher was so mad, his cheeks puffed out and looked redder than the geraniums hanging in the window.

"You two get out of here and leave me and my friend alone!"

"Sure pet—don't fret—we'll be gone before they get the net . . ." sang Cindy.

"Oh clever, Cindy," said Carol, "clever, clever, clever. I really like that."

I forgot about my snack. I could see by the

kitchen clock that it was almost time for *Space 3000*, but I didn't say anything. I could tell Christopher hated to be teased by his sisters but they sure were funny to watch.

Cindy poured half a bag of potato chips into a bowl and Carol grabbed pretzel sticks. They poured themselves glasses of milk and I counted at least three teaspoons of chocolate syrup apiece.

They walked out loaded with their snacks and Cindy yelled to me, "Listen kid, if you want some potato chips just take them. Otherwise fatso here will grab them all for himself."

Christopher yelled back, "Get out of here." The girls just laughed. Carol blew three kisses in the air. Her lips were all chocolatey. Benjie might be mean sometimes but at least he doesn't slobber all over me.

"Do you want some chips, Wilson?" Christopher's face was still red.

"I'll have a couple. But I'm really not supposed to eat them because of cholesterol."

"Cholesterol?" Christopher didn't understand.

"I told you my mother's a nurse. Well, she says you shouldn't eat snacks that are fatty and greasy."

Christopher munched on. "Why not?"

I didn't want Christopher to get mad and sit on me especially since he likes *Space 3000*. But from the looks of him and the twins, they must eat a lot of fat. "See, Christopher, these snacks make fat

56

globules when you eat them. And it's not good to have fat in your blood, because when you're older you can have a heart attack."

"How old?"

"I don't know, about sixteen, maybe."

Christopher put down the potato chips and pushed the bowl away. "How come you're always talking about heart attacks, Wilson?"

"Hi Chris, did you have a snack?" I turned around. Another blonde girl and she looked just like everyone else. "Hi, I'm Clarissa, Christopher's oldest sister." She turned to him. "Are the twins home yet?"

"Can't you hear them screeching upstairs?"

She opened the pantry and took out a chocolate bar. "I hope you kids didn't eat everything up. I'm having some friends over later." This certainly was an eating family. I wondered what Christopher's father says when he sees the cash register tapes from the supermarket. My dad yells when he sees ours and we're just four skinny people who don't even eat any cholesterol.

"We're going in the den to watch TV," Christopher told his sister.

"Don't make a mess, I'm not cleaning up after you." When we left the kitchen Clarissa was spooning chocolate syrup into her milk.

I shook my head. "Do you have any more sisters, Christopher?"

"What are you, a wise guy, Wilson? Three pains are enough."

*Space 3000* had been on about five minutes. "Darn it," said Christopher. "We missed the first two commercials. They might have had some good stuff to send away for." He opened a closet and came out with a helmet.

"Wow, Christopher! You sent away for a Captain Future helmet? My mom said it was too expensive."

Christopher put it on. "I got it last summer when I drove my mother crazy itching my chicken pox." He was lucky. I got pink smelly calomine lotion for my itches.

"Can I try it?" I asked.

"Sure." He handed me the space helmet. It was neat. I pulled down the clear plastic top that covered the face. There were air holes near the nose so you could breathe.

"You fix the antennae like this." Christopher reached around the back and pulled apart the metal wires.

"Calling planet Alpha, calling Alpha." I spoke through the voice box.

"Alpha answering. Alpha answering." Christopher made a fist in front of his mouth like a microphone and spoke into it. He walked around me and tapped the helmet. "If that dumb school didn't make us take injections for the mumps, I might have caught them this year. Then I could have sent away for a set of laser guns. My mother goes bananas when I'm sick."

The TV was blasting. Captain Future was ready to leave his big starship and go exploring in a little space racer. "You wear the helmet until the next commercial," said Christopher. "Then I'll put it on."

We sat on the floor. Christopher could imitate the rocket take-off. "Vavabooommmmennnnzzoo-ooooom. Vavavavaboommmmmenenezooom." His hands shot up in the air like a rocket.

I pushed back the plastic visor. On *Space 3000* they had air-conditioned helmets; this one was pretty sweaty.

A commercial came on, showing a starship just like Captain Future's. It was too expensive. You couldn't even save up cereal tops for part of it. They wanted money.

"That's neat," said Christopher. "But I'd probably have to have one of those heart attacks you were talking about to get my mother to buy one of them."

"We could make one." I took the helmet off. Christopher put it on.

"Do you think so?"

"My father has wood in the basement. He'd

give us some and we could glue it together."

"Yeah, and I have lots of paints left over from model sets."

We looked back at the TV. Captain Future was ready to sign off. A voice yelled from the doorway, "Beat it, kids, because my friends are coming." It was Clarissa.

"Aren't you too big to be playing soldier?" she asked Christopher.

"I'm not playing soldier." But he pulled off the helmet.

"Well, get outside." And Clarissa stood with her arms folded until we shut off the TV and left the room.

"They drive me crazy in this house," Christopher said as we walked back into the living room. "Just listen to that music. Cindy plays her radio, Clarissa plays the stereo, and Carol plays tapes and they all play different songs at the same time. You could go nuts around here."

"My brother's a pain sometimes too," I said. "He lifts weights."

"Does he do it to music?" asked Christopher.

I shook my head no.

"It's too late to start our model," said Christopher. "Maybe we can do it next week."

"O.K. You come to my house next time." That's what you do when you're friends, change off houses. I'd have to remember to ask Mom to buy chocolate syrup and cupcakes.

One of the twins walked in. I looked at her collar. It was Cindy. "Hey, Christopher, you better be careful if you go outside. Don't spoil your voice. We've got to sing tonight."

Christopher was crawling around the couch looking for his softball glove. A softball was in the corner by a lamp.

"Hey, kid, what's your name again?" she asked.

I pointed to myself. "Me?"

"Well, there's no one else in the room."

"Joshua."

"Yeah, hey, Joshua, did Christopher tell you what a great singer he was?"

"Shut up, Cindy."

"We all are. Singers, I mean. They call us The Six C Notes. Sometimes Christopher gets too embarrassed to tell anybody."

"Quit it, Cindy."

She continued. "There's Christopher and I'm Cindy and there's Carol and Clarissa and my father's name is Charles and my mother is Connie."

I still didn't get it except that somebody liked the letter C.

"Our mother used to be a singer and she was hoping we'd have good voices, so she named us all with C's so we could have a singing group."

Christopher had picked up my *Space 3000* magazines. "Don't listen to her, Josh. Can I keep the magazines and see which ones I want to trade?"

"Sure."

Boy, you couldn't tell about people. When Christopher was sitting on Peter Benson to make him stop saying Jelly Belly, I sure wouldn't have thought he was a singer.

"Do you sing on TV, Cindy?"

Christopher was tugging on my arm. "Come on out. No, we don't sing on TV, just at church or some ladies clubs or PAL dances. And you better not tell any of the kids in school or I'll slug you."

We ran out. "I'll throw you some fly balls, Joshua, so you don't stand like such a klutz next time you're in the outfield."

I never knew a family singing group. Once my grandmother took me to see *The Sound of Music*. And in that picture the whole family started singing as they climbed over mountains to escape from the Nazis. Too bad there weren't any enemies around here that Christopher's family could sing and escape from.

I figured maybe I should tell Christopher about the Czar.

"Hey, Christopher, do you know where I go on Tuesdays?"

"Where?"

"To the Hillside Home for the Aged."

Christopher winged the ball right past me. I had to run it down. He said, "Gee, it's too bad you have to go. Just passing that place gives me the creeps."

He punched his glove. "Now when I throw the ball this time, make believe you're Captain Flash and this is the moon. So you got no gravity to hold you down and the ball will float in the air until you catch it."

# 8

As soon as I saw Christopher Monday morning, I asked if he wanted to come over and start our space starship.

"Sorry, Wilson. I promised the guys I'd stay in the playground after school and get a game up."

"That's O.K."

"But look." He opened his notebook. "I've been drawing pictures of what I think our starship should look like." Sure enough, Christopher had about six pages of paper covered with starship sketches. He gave them to me. "You keep 'em and see what you like and maybe we can start to work in a couple of days."

I tried to work on the pictures after school, while I was watching *Space 3000*. But it wasn't as much fun as when we both watched together. Even when I got the vavavavavabooommmmmmmmzooooooooommmmmmm sound pretty good.

On Tuesday, when the bell rang for dismissal, I didn't care what anybody was doing. Even Christopher. I couldn't wait to see the Czar. My mother and I made a deal. She waited for me by the Dairy Queen. I could run in and get an ice cream for my snack and nobody would call me a baby for having my mother pick me up.

I had almost forgotten the smell of the Home until my eyes started to sting. I wondered if the old guys walked around rubbing eyes all day. Today there was another smell. And it wasn't cooking. Even Mother sniffed. "I think they've started painting some of the rooms, Josh."

That was it. Fresh paint. Phew, paint scrunched your whole face up. "Wait here a minute." Mother walked into Dr. Corby's office.

"Watch out, little boy, eyes front!" A nurse was pushing a patient in a wheelchair. They should have signal lights like cars do.

Mother came out. "The lounge is being painted, Josh, so most of the patients are in their rooms." She looked worried. "Now what am I going to do with you?"

"Can't I go to Mr. Romanoff's room, Mother? He's the one I want to visit anyway."

"Fine." She steered me down the hall by my

65

shoulders. We met Mrs. Horowitz. "Hello, Joshua. It's nice to see you again." She still smelled like peppermints. Mother later told me it was linament, for her arthritis.

"Did I ever show you a picture of my grandson?" She didn't wait for me to answer, just reached into her pocket and pulled out a picture. She must sure show her grandson to a lot of people to get that picture so wrinkled. She unfolded it, held it up, folded it, and put it back in her pocket. I didn't get to see anything but the wrinkles! "It's too bad you can't play piano today. I hope you'll play for us when the room's all painted. We just love music."

I didn't answer. I hoped they painted the floor after the walls and then the ceiling and then maybe the walls would be dirty again so they could start over and I'd never have to play. At least not until I learned a new song. Mother gave me a little pinch on the ear. That was her secret signal to speak up and not act shy.

"I'll come back and play again, Mrs. Horowitz." Maybe I didn't want another pinch on the ear because then I said, "Mrs. Horowitz, I'm not so good at music. But I have a friend, Christopher, whose whole family is a singing group called The Six C Notes. I'll ask Christopher and his family to come sing for you."

"Did you hear that?" Mrs. Horowitz hugged me and smiled at Mother.

As soon as the words were out of my mouth I felt a jumping bean in the bottom of my stomach. Whatever made me say it? Christopher hadn't even come over to my house yet. And he thought the Home for the Aged was creepy. Besides I had promised him I wouldn't tell anybody about The Six C Notes. Well, not anybody, just the kids in school. Maybe Mrs. Horowitz would forget.

Mother and I kept walking. She gave me a squeeze. "Joshua, that was so nice of you. I didn't know Christopher had a singing family. That would be terrific of them to sing for the Home." The bean in my stomach was really hopping all over. Mrs. Horowitz might forget. Mother wouldn't!

We stopped in front of Room 25. "That's his," said Mother.

The door was closed. I put my ear next to it. I heard loud counting. "Twenty-three, twenty-four, twenty-five, twenty-six . . ." I rubbed the jumping part of my stomach and knocked on the door.

"Come!" boomed the Czar.

"I'll see you later." Mother started down the hall.

"What room will you be in?" I wanted to know

where she was in case I had to make a quick getaway.

"I'll be in Physical Therapy. We'll meet at 5 o'clock."

I pushed open the door. Instead of a face I saw a pair of black boots waving in the air. There were the boots, then the black pants and the shirt flopping over the Czar's belly.

"Vell. Don't stand there. Close door. Vat's the matter, you never saw anyvone stand on head before?"

Sure enough, the Czar was on his head, straight as could be. *"Ochin Khorosho*, very good. It's my cavalryman Joshua. Come! Sit on floor so I can see you."

"Why are you standing on your head, Mr. Romanoff?"

"Vhy am I standing on my head? Vhy am I standing on my head? All great military men stood on heads. Napoleon, George Vashington. It makes blood rush to brains and helps you think!"

"Oh!" I sat on the floor. It was still hard to see the Czar's upside down face. I lay down on my belly. Now we were eye to eye. Something else was funny. The Czar was upside down but his long white beard wasn't falling over his face. It was stiff and straight, pointed right at the ceiling.

"How come your beard isn't falling over?" I asked.

The Czar's bushy eyebrows bunched across his nose. "How come, you ask? How come? A good soldier, he is observant. You tell me."

I looked real close. "I see." The Czar had wound the edge of his beard around a button on his shirt. That kept it straight even though the rest of him was upside down.

"Vell, Joshua, tell me. Vat you been doing all veek long?"

The Czar was like a general asking for a report. So I gave him one. I told him about Benjie and the weights and about the kids calling me Klutz and even about Christopher and The Six C Notes. The jumping bean in my stomach began again when I told how I promised Mrs. Horowitz that The Six C Notes would sing here. Only a real klutz would do that!

The Czar turned right side up. He sat on the bed and patted a place next to him. The bed was hard and I wiggled around trying to get comfortable. There was nothing in the room but the skinny bed, a night table and a straight chair, and of course that germ smell. I didn't see my picture anyplace. Maybe he hadn't gotten it. Maybe he didn't think it was good enough to keep.

"I looked on the globe, Mr. Romanoff, but I couldn't find Markovo."

"*Nyet!* You couldn't find Markovo?" The Czar jumped up. "Vell, how you think I lost my toe van-dering all over Siberia? I couldn't find either. All because of my miserable cousin."

There was a shiny sword in the corner I hadn't seen before. I wondered if that was the sword that cut his toe off!

The Czar sighed. "I show you something." He opened the drawer to his night table. There were lots of papers and junk all thrown together. I was glad Mother wasn't here. She made you throw out stuff no matter how much you wanted to keep it.

"Aha, here it is!" The Czar held a little dirty twig. He handed it to me. It wasn't a twig, it was a bone. An old dried-out bone. The loser's half of a chicken wishbone. I know because every Friday night after chicken dinner, Benjie and I take hold of the wishbone, make a wish, and pull. This is the half I always get.

The Czar took the wishbone back and rolled it between his fingers. He leaned back against the pillow. "Ven I vas little boy in Russia, my cousins and I alvays vent in summer to large dacha on Black Sea."

"A dacha?" I asked.

"Country house. Ve vould svim and hunt and play games. My father and Czar of Russia vere cousins. I used to fight all the time with Nicholas who vas Czaravitch."

"But your name is Nicholas, Mr. Romanoff."

"Yah, all royal boys in Russia named Nicholas.

But the Czaravitch vas Prince. He vas supposed to be Czar after his fater."

"Like the Prince in England."

The Czar pulled his beard. "You talk too much. You vant to hear story or not?"

"I'm sorry." I don't usually talk so much. I crossed my fingers so I would remember not to ask questions.

"Anyvay, von day, Czaravitch Nicholas and I vere wrestling. Our faters came to vatch. I had Nicholas pinned down to the ground. He vas crying."

"I don't blame him." My fingers had come uncrossed. "Sometimes I cry too, when Benjie wrestles me."

BAM! I had forgotten about the riding stick. The Czar slammed it down on the night table. I crossed the fingers on both hands to help keep me quiet.

"So our two faters vere cheering us on. That night at supper the Czar called for quiet. He called me and Czaravitch to come to head table. He said he vas sad. His son vouldn't beat me in wrestling. But he vas going to give him von more chance. Ve vere eating roasted chicken and Czar pulled out this very chicken bone. He took my right thumb and the Czaravitch's thumb and placed them on either side of vishbone. Than he made announcement. 'Whoever breaks off larger piece of vishbone vill be Czar of Russia. Loser vill be Czar of Mar-kovo.' "

I couldn't keep still. "You mean he was going to take Russia away from his very own son if he lost the wishbone contest?"

"That's right. He alvays liked contests."

The Czar looked at the half of wishbone in his hand. "I vas best rider, best wrestler, best swords-man in all Russia. But I could not get my thumb right on the vishbone and SNAP, my cousin broke it, got the vinning half, and von all of Russia. Vich of course didn't do him too much good later on. As for me . . ." He shrugged his shoulders and put the piece of wishbone back in the night table. "I got stuck vith Markovo. Vich I couldn't never find."

Now I leaned back on the bed. "Wow, I'll bet nobody in the whole world knows that story. Not even the people who write the history books."

"True. True." The Czar stood up. Now he picked up the sword and waved it up and down in the air. I moved as close to the wall as I could to get away from that swinging sword.

"Just think." Swish, swish. That sword was really moving. "A whole Empire lost on vish-bone." He finally put the sword down and looked at me.

"But now ve take care of Joshua."

"Me?"

He picked up his riding stick again. "Yes, you! I start collecting chicken vishbones."

"Chicken wishbones?"

"Tell me, Joshua. You say you make vish vith your brother on the vishbone. Who vins?"

I didn't have to think about it. "Benjie always wins. That's because he's stronger."

"See vat I mean? Ve start vith chicken vishbones. They make chicken every Sunday and chicken soup every Thursday here. I put vord out to kitchen. Next time you come, ve practice snapping chicken bones." He shook my hand, got off the bed, and stood on his head again. "You go now and meet that pretty mama of yours."

"But Mr. Czar, chicken wishbones?"

He was standing straight as a stick, upside down. "I see you next veek. No more kingdoms lost because of vishbones." He raised one hand and pointed to the closet. His body didn't even shake. "Open door, Joshua."

I opened the door. The picture I had drawn was hanging on the back. It was framed with bright red ribbon that matched the uniforms on the soldiers. You couldn't even see the dirty footprint.

"Not allowed to make holes in room valls. You go now, Joshua. I see you next veek. My brain is tired. I rest it now." He closed his eyes tightly and waved his legs in the air. I tiptoed out of the room.

# 9

AFTER SUPPER, I got out my extra credit library book and hunched over the desk. I kept my head down and tried to make believe I didn't see Benjie with all his barbells in the middle of the room.

It didn't work. "C'mon, Joshua. Close that book. On your feet." Benjie had the large bar out and he was screwing five-pound weights into each side. It looked like we were going to work on arm muscles again. I think Benjie decided to make developing muscles his life's work. Sometimes I think it's better when he ignores me.

"Do I have to? My arms still hurt from yesterday."

"Are the kids still calling you Klutz?"

"Not everybody . . ."

"Off that chair. You're not even half built up."

Benjie reached down and picked up the barbell. "Watch me!" He lifted it over his head and kept his arms and elbows perfectly straight. Then he bent over, still holding the bar, and touched the floor without bending his knees. He took a deep breath, stood up, and held it over his head again. He did it ten times in a row, then flexed his arm muscle for me. "Feel this," he said. I could feel the muscle right through his T-shirt.

"Now it's your turn."

I bent over and picked up the weights. Every night they felt heavier and heavier. Benjie told me they would start to feel light. I got the bar to my waist and tried to lift it over my head. My back was bent and I couldn't straighten my elbow. I started to count. "One . . ."

"*Stop!*" Benjie yelled. "Your elbows are bent. Straighten your arms."

"Nobody can do it perfect."

"I can. And you could too if you weren't such a nerd!"

My shoulders felt as if they were going to fall off. I tried again. I don't know how Benjie thought his yelling was going to help me lift that bar. But this time I got it up in the air. My arms and elbows were straight too. But when I bent over to touch the floor the bar fell out of my hands. I sat down and wiped my hands on my pants.

"No resting. You only did one. Nine more to go!"

"I can't, Benjie, I'm pooped!"

"You want muscles in your arms, you lift weights. If you keep sitting you'll get muscles in your . . ."

I stood up. My arms were shaking. "How am I going to be able to play ball? My arms are so sore, I won't even be able to throw."

"Did your legs hurt last week?"

"Yeah."

"Well, they stopped hurting, didn't they?"

I had to agree. They stopped hurting, but I didn't notice that they worked any better when I had to run around bases. Benjie handed me the weights. I was just about to say, "I can't," when I remembered something.

"Benjie, I'll be right back."

"Where you going now?"

"I forgot to tell Mom something."

"Well, hurry up." He lifted the barbell with one hand and pounded his chest like Tarzan with the other one. "I'll be waiting for you!"

Mom and Dad were watching TV. "Hey, Mom, do you think we could have roast chicken for dinner tomorrow night?"

"Why, I guess so. Any special reason?"

"No, I just feel like having chicken." I turned to

go back to my room. "And could you make sure that the chicken has a wishbone in it?"

I saw Mom look across at Dad, who just shrugged his shoulders. "Well," she said, "I guess I never cooked a chicken that didn't have one."

"Thanks, Mom. But just double check before you cook it."

It was cooler in the morning, but the sun was still shining. I tried to test the air by making steam with my breath. When it was time for gym Mr. Magliore popped his head into the classroom. "Coats and jackets, gang. I think we can catch another day outdoors."

I almost got trampled as the kids ran for their coats. My windbreaker was on the floor. I took as long as I could to zip it. I wonder if the Board of Health knows that Mr. Magliore is still taking us out. In current events we talked about flu season and keeping out of drafts. It would be a nice thing if the whole fourth grade of Deerfield School came down with the flu from playing outside. He'd probably lose his job.

Mr. Magliore was talking to Miss Garett. She went to get her coat. "I think I'll go out with you today, class, and get some fresh air." None of the other grade teachers went with their classes to gym period.

Marjorie shoved me as I got on line. "I think Miss Garett wants fresh air and Mr. Magliore." She pushed me again. "Get it, Klutz, they are in LOVE!" I got it. You would think if Mr. Magliore was in love he would be worried about Miss Garett getting the flu, even if he didn't care about us.

I crossed my fingers on the way out. I hoped we would chose by onesies, twosies today instead of Captains.

Mr. Magliore made us line up. All our breath was coming out like steam. I could puff in and out and make little smoky animals in the air. I hopped on one foot, then the other. It was really cold. Miss Garett didn't have all her coat buttons closed. Maybe being in love made you feel warmer. Christopher was whispering to me, "He's calling you, Joshua."

It was Captains. Mr. Magliore blew his whistle twice. "The two captains for today are Joshua Wilson and Sue Peterson." I didn't move. Maybe he called out the wrong name. Marjorie gave me a shove. "Go ahead, you're CAPTAIN!"

I had to stand next to Sue. She was looking the class over.

Everybody was yelling.

"Choose me. Choose me."

"I want to be on Sue's team."

"C'mon, Sue. Pick me."

I always thought Mr. Magliore was my friend. Why did he make me captain?

Sue picked Marjorie. Everybody yelled. Now it

was my turn. My hands were sweating inside my pockets but my mouth was all dry. The kids were making so much noise, I could hardly think.

"Let's go, Joshua," said Mr. Magliore.

Peter Benson was yelling from the line. "Hey, Wilson, pick me, Wilson."

Mr. Magliore blew his whistle. "Will you all be quiet? Joshua's the captain. He'll pick whoever he wants to." He smiled and gave me a wink. "But come on, Josh, time's a-wasting, make your first pick."

I looked at the line again. All I saw were waving hands. Waving hands and finally Christopher's face. I took my hands out of my pocket. "I pick Christopher."

The kids started to yell at Sue again. Christopher ran to stand behind me. "O.K. Wilson, who are you going to pick next?"

"You help me choose. You know how the kids play better than I do."

"O.K. We'll see who Sue picks."

And we did. Sue picked. Then Christopher and I would whisper together and I'd pick. Finally there were two teams. Our team was in the outfield first. Mr. Magliore handed me the ball. Usually the captain of the team got to be the pitcher. "O.K. Josh," he said. "Get your team out in their positions."

Christopher was already lining everyone up. I

walked to the pitcher's mound. Christopher and I tossed the ball back and forth a few times. I thought about Captain Future. Whenever he had a mission to perform, he picked the best of his crew. "Christopher, would you pitch? My shoulders hurt from all my weight lifting. I don't think I can pitch yet."

"Sure." Christopher grabbed the ball. "Josh, you go play the outfield."

I ran to my position. Mr. Magliore came over to me. "Aren't you going to pitch, Joshua?"

"No, I want to be in the outfield, Mr. Magliore."

"Joshua, you're captain, so you can play any position you want to. No one on the team can tell you what to do."

"I know, Mr. Magliore, but can't I still be captain even if I'm in the outfield?"

Mr. Magliore slapped me on the shoulder. *Ow!* It wasn't his fault, he didn't know I'd been lifting weights. "Why I guess you can, Joshua Wilson. I guess you can be captain from any darn position you want."

Today was the double gym period that Mr. Magliore had promised. I watched Christopher pitch. No balls came to the outfield. Miss Garett called out the score. "Sue's team—zero. Joshua's team—zero." It was fun to be captain.

I got up to bat three times. The first two times I

struck out. The third time Sue hit me with a pitched ball so I walked to first. I waved to Christopher who was telling the rest of the team how to hit.

He ran over to me. We whispered so Peter Benson wouldn't hear. "Remember Joshua, watch the batter and when he hits, run as fast as you can."

The next batter hit a grounder to the outfield. I ran to second base. I made it in plenty of time and jumped twice on the base just to prove I was there. I was warmed up now. A lot of the kids had taken off their jackets. I unzipped mine. I waved to Mr. Magliore and Miss Garett so they would be sure to see me on second base.

Now we had a runner on first, I was on second, and Andy was up at bat. Christopher was yelling all kinds of instructions. I watched the batter real hard. My heart was thumping. I could score a run. I bent my legs like Benjie taught me. Andy swung hard at the ball. I watched the ball fly away from the bat. It was going, going, gone. Way up in the sky, just like they say on TV. I started running. I pumped my legs and went as fast as I could. I touched third base and passed it. I didn't look up, just kept running. My legs were really working. I could hear screaming, but I couldn't tell what it was. I just wanted to make it to home plate.

I did it. Across home plate! I could hardly catch

my breath and my heart was pounding all the way up to my ears. But I was over the plate. I was a run batted in. Marjorie was the catcher. She was yelling and laughing. I couldn't understand what she was saying. "Joshua, you KLUTZ, you KLUTZ, you're out!"

How could I be out? Nobody had tagged me. My ears were still buzzing from my fast run. She pointed to second base. Sue was standing there with the ball. "Look, look out there." Sue held the ball up. Andy's hit hadn't been a home run. It was a long pop fly and the outfielder had caught it. I had never looked back to see if the ball had been caught. I was too busy running. And now I was out because I hadn't gone back to second base.

I zipped up my jacket and went to the sidelines. I could still hear Marjorie yelling, "KLUTZ." Christopher came over. "Don't worry, Josh, you're only the second out. We can still score."

I felt cold again. I didn't want to talk because I was afraid I'd cry and then the class would really give it to me.

Christopher made the Captain Future friendship sign. "Don't listen to Marjorie. She can drive you crazy, just like my sisters."

There were two more innings. Christopher hit a triple in the last inning and my team won by two runs. Mr. Magliore tried to congratulate me, but I just rubbed my sneakers in the dirt. I hadn't really been the captain. If Christopher hadn't picked everybody and pitched, we never would have won.

That night, right before dinner, I got another one of those telephone calls. The giggles and then the voice squeaking, "JOSHUA WILSON IS A KLUTZ!"

I just pushed the pieces of chicken around my plate. "What's the matter, Josh?" asked Mother. "I made the chicken especially for you and you've hardly touched it." She reached over to feel my forehead. I guess her hand is better than any doctor's thermometer. "I hope you're not coming down with something."

Dad had a piece of the chicken breast on his plate. He held something up. "Hey, Josh, here's the wishbone. Didn't you ask for it?"

Benjie reached for it. "Give it to me, Dad. C'mon, Josh, I'll make a wish with you."

I looked at the bone. It still had some pieces of white meat on it. "No, I don't feel like making a wish tonight."

"O.K." Benjie grabbed for it again. "C'mon, Dad, you and me'll make a wish."

Mom took the bone away from Dad. "I'll keep it. We'll put it on the window sill to dry out and then you can make a wish when you feel like it. O.K. Josh?"

That was a better idea. I took a bite of chicken.

After the day I had today, I wasn't going to take any chances. I'd wait for next week. No sense wasting my chicken bone wish until I had time to practice with the Czar!

# 10

CHRISTOPHER AND I made a date to start our starship on Thursday. I picked Thursday because I
knew Benjie had soccer practice. I didn't want him
around making wisecracks about Captain Future.
Mother stocked up on chocolate cupcakes, even
though she doesn't like us to eat sweets.

We walked home together. I said "Hi" to every
kid I saw as we walked out of the playground. I
wanted to make sure they knew Christopher was
going home with me.

Mother was home. I introduced Christopher. I
saw her look at his belly roll. "Joshua," she said,
"there's extra cupcakes in the cake box, if you need
them."

Christopher ate five cupcakes. First he ate the icing all around and then finished the cake down to the last crumb. He had two glasses of milk. But that's because we don't have tall glasses like at his house.

"Thanks for the cake, Mrs. Wilson."

"You're welcome, Christopher."

Mother was smiling. She always likes polite kids.

"What bakery do you go to, Mrs. Wilson?"

"The one on Millburn Avenue."

"Oh, my mom goes to the one on Livingston. They make things special for us." Christopher slurped the last drop of milk from his glass. "Dad says we must have put the baker's kids through college by now."

"I'll bet you have, Christopher. I'll bet you have."

"C'mon, Christopher." I didn't want to sit around talking about bakeries all day. "It's just about time for *Space 3000* and I got the wood and everything ready."

Christopher followed me into the den. Mother had spread newspapers on the floor so we could work without making a mess.

Christopher turned on the TV. *Space 3000* was just starting. "Do you have any snacks in here?" He looked around.

"No, if we want something, we can walk into the kitchen."

"O.K. but that way we'll waste time. If you bring it here, we won't have to stop."

I went back into the kitchen and poured some pretzels into a bowl. Mother had peeled carrot sticks for me.

"Why don't you try a carrot?" I asked Christopher.

"Rabbit food." And he grabbed a handful of pretzels. As he ate, he pressed a finger into my chest. "That's why you're so skinny and don't have muscles. You don't eat anything that sticks to your ribs."

I heard on TV that cereal sticks to your ribs but I never thought about pretzels. I guess they must. Something's sticking to Christopher's ribs about four layers deep.

I had plywood from Dad's workshop. Christopher had brought over some big pieces of cardboard. We watched *Space 3000* and especially studied the starship. When the program was over, we turned off the TV. Christopher got down on his hands and knees.

"Did you save my pictures, Joshua?"

I got out the pictures he had drawn last week and handed him a marking pencil. Very carefully he drew the shape of the starship on the cardboard. It was going to be a pattern. Like when a lady makes a dress. Then we'd take the cardboard and trace it on the wood and my father would cut it out for us with his power saw.

When Christopher finished, he sat back on his heels. I took the scissors and cut around the cardboard on the black lines he had made. He ate while I cut. "You know something, Joshua, we make a good team."

I ate my carrot sticks while he drew the back of the ship on the second piece of cardboard. Then I cut it out. We had the front and back ready for the saw.

"You know, Christopher, if we finish this really good, maybe we can enter it in the science fair."

"Yeah. We don't have to say it's Captain Future's ship. We can call it The Space Traveler."

"Hi, Mom." I heard Benjie in the kitchen. What was he doing home so early? He came into the den and pointed to Christopher.

"Who's that?"

"It's my friend Christopher."

"What are you doing?"

Christopher answered, "We're making a spaceship for the science fair." Christopher's pretty smart. He realized that Benjie would tease us just like his sisters do if he thought we were playing Captain Future.

"That's pretty neat. Let me see." Benjie never

thinks anything I do is pretty neat. He got down on the floor and looked at the cardboard cut-outs.

"Why don't you make two holes in the back of the ship?" He pointed to the place. "We've got an old automobile muffler in the basement. Ask Dad, Josh. I'll bet he'd let you have it. You could stick it in the holes and it'd act like your exhaust pipes for the rocket engine."

"Hey, that's a great idea," said Christopher. "Thanks."

Benjie stood up. "After you paint the wood, you should shellac it, to make it look real shiny."

Sometimes Benjie does know an awful lot. "Thanks, Benjie," I said.

He got up. "But don't touch any of my brushes or I'll rearrange your ears." He jumped up and down and moved his fists as if he were boxing.

I could hear him yell when he got back into the kitchen. "Who ate all the chocolate cupcakes? I'll bet it was that fat kid who's playing with Joshua!"

Mom was trying to shush him, but if Christopher heard he didn't pay any attention. He was busy drawing the two holes in the back of the ship for the exhaust pipes.

I called Dad at his office and he promised to cut out the ship that night on his power saw. Before Christopher left we made a date to glue the ship together next week at his house.

"I saw this ad on TV, Joshua. One drop of glue

was holding up an army tank that was attached by a chain to a helicopter."

"I saw that ad too. But my mother broke a real good plate and my dad used the glue and it didn't even hold the thin little plate together."

"Well, it must just be for extra heavy jobs."

"We can try it on our ship anyway."

Mother came into the den.

"Goodbye, Mrs. Wilson."

"Goodbye, Christopher, come again."

"So long, Christopher, I'll see you tomorrow."

"Sure thing, Wilson." And we gave each other the Captain Future friendship signal before he left.

I got two more of those telephone calls during the week. In school I drew a chart of the class and tried to figure out who it was. I really suspected Marjorie. But even though she was a rat, she wasn't sneaky. She called me Klutz right to my face. It could be Peter Benson or Andy. It could be almost anyone. The only kid I was sure of was Christopher.

I could hardly wait for Tuesday to come around again. I thought about calling the Czar, but I didn't know the number. And he doesn't have a phone in his room. Old Dr. Corby would call him into the office and then he'd be able to listen to our conversation. I kept hoping the Czar had been able to get some chicken bones.

When I woke up Tuesday morning, I knew my

luck had changed. It was raining. Our class stayed inside and played dodge ball. I got to wear the whistle and be the referee twice. I sidelined Marjorie once.

At the end of class, Mr. Magliore made an announcement. "This fourth grade has been so well behaved that we're going to take a special field trip next week." I was twirling the whistle.

"Miss Garett and I have decided . . ." When he said "Miss Garett," Marjorie covered her mouth and giggled. Christopher kicked her in the foot where it wouldn't show. Mr. Magliore continued. "Miss Garett and I have decided that we will take the class on a hike to the South Mountain Reservation."

The class cheered. I had been to the reservation with my family. It's lots of fun. There's fields for games and barbecuing and lots of mountain trails.

Mr. Magliore blew his whistle again for quiet. "We'll go for a hike, picnic out in the woods, and collect leaves, seeds, and rock specimens for your science table. Everyone be prepared with warm sweaters or sweat suits."

I was happy. It was Tuesday. The class was going on a trip next week. Marjorie was rubbing her ankle where Christopher had kicked her. And Mr. Magliore never even mentioned softball.

# 11

THE CZAR was waiting in the front lobby. Actually he was marching back and forth in his black shiny boots, waving his riding stick.

"Joshua! I been vaiting for you. Hello, Mrs. Vilson." He clicked his heels and bowed toward Mother. He took her hand and kissed it, just like in those old movies. "Ve go, Joshua. They still painting here."

Phew! He didn't have to tell me. My nose was already curling.

"Mrs. Vilson, ve see you later. Joshua and I have important business to attend to. Ve be in my room."

I just had a second to wave good-bye to Mom

before he grabbed my hand and pulled me down the hall.

"Come, ve hurry. Mrs. Horovitz looking for you. She vants to show you her grandson's picture."

"But she shows me every week."

"No matter, everybody has to see picture of her grandson."

"But she wrinkles it all up from showing it so many times."

"That's all right. Ven she uses it up, she cut another picture of little boy out of paper."

"You mean that's really not her grandson?"

The Czar shrugged his shoulders. "Who knows? Maybe every little boy's picture is her grandson."

Before I could figure that out, the Czar opened the door to Number 25 and pushed me inside. He took out a cardboard sign that had a string attached. The sign said, "Don't DESTERB!"

He hung it on the outside door knob and shut the door tightly.

"Come here." He pulled me over to the window sill. I could hardly believe my eyes. I was worried about him getting one chicken bone. There must have been forty-five chicken wishbones drying on the sill! He rubbed his hands together. "Aha, all veek, everyvone, I told them must save me chicken vishbone. See, they are all beautiful. Before ve begin, Joshua, you make vish."

"But I thought we were just practicing?"

"Ve are. But vat if you break off vinning side? You've got to have vish ready just in case. Close your eyes."

I closed them.

"You can't see, can you?" asked the Czar.

"No." I shook my head. There were only the little dancing light spots that you see when you scrunch your eyes together very tightly.

"Now cross your fingers." I did. "Now cross your ankles." I did. "Now cross your wrists together." I started to twist my wrists but the Czar yelled, "*Nyet!* Cross wrists, but still keep fingers crossed." I recrossed my fingers. It seems as if it's as hard to make a wish as it is to play ball. Finally I was in the right position.

"*Ochin Khorosho,* very good. Now vish as hard as you can." I took a deep breath. I wished as hard as I could and felt the wish go through my wrists and fingers and even down to my crossed ankles.

"O.K., now ve practice."

I sat on the bed. The Czar picked out a chicken wishbone. He held one end out to me. "Let me see you try to vin bigger half." I grabbed onto the wishbone and pulled. It broke. I looked down. I had the smaller half. The Czar took down another.

The same thing happened. And another. And another. The score was: the Czar five winning wishbone pieces and zero for me.

I took off my sweater. Maybe I was too klutzy to even learn how to break chicken wishbones.

The Czar shook his finger. "You must try harder. You lost five vishes already."

He pulled over the one chair in the room. Then he put the night table in between the bed and the chair. He told me to sit on the chair. He stayed on the bed.

"Now Joshua, I show you how. Put your elbow on the table." I did. "Now sit up nice and straight. Make a fist." I followed all the directions. "Now open your fist ven I give you vishbone. Put your thumb on your side real hard."

The Czar picked out a large wishbone. "Now close your fist around your half of vishbone. Dig your elbow into table and vun, two, three, PPPPUUUUUUUULLLLLLLL . . ."

I did. I looked down. I still had the shorter piece.

"Never mind. That vas better. Ve try again. Ven I say three, you pull up vith your thumb vith all your might. Vun, two, three, PPPPPPPPPPP-UUUUUUUUUUUUUUUUULLLLLLLLLL . . ." No good. I still had the smaller piece. Well, one thing for sure, the Czar didn't believe in letting kids win just to make them feel good. I looked at the window sill. There were a lot of wishbones left. I put my elbow on the table.

"Vun, two, three, PPPPPPPPPPPUUUUUUUUUUU-UUUUULLLLLLLLL . . ."

"Vun, two, three, PPPPPPPPPPPUUUUUUUUUUU-UUUUULLLLLLLLL . . ."

The Czar reached for another wishbone. "Wait a minute, Mr. Romanoff." I jumped up. "I won that time." The bigger half was in my hand. "Look, I got it. I got it!"

"Vat? Let me see." The Czar looked at the piece of bone in my hand. He saw it too. I had the winner's piece. He slapped me on the back. "You see, you did it. I told you." I looked down at the winning piece. I really had broken it. Fair and square.

The Czar slapped me again. "Now you keep it alvays in pocket for luck." He stood up. "Ve have toast now."

I closed my eyes as I put the wishbone in my pocket. I waited to feel different. Like when you have a birthday and expect to feel a year older. No, I still felt like the same old Joshua. Maybe wishes and good luck take a little while to work.

The Czar opened his closet door. My picture was still hanging there. Clothes and packages fell into the room. He kicked things aside and went hunting in the bottom of his closet. He threw out a silk blouse like the one he was wearing except it was black with fancy red stitches. Out came some old newspapers that had funny printing. I couldn't read it even though I'm in the Stage Four Bionic Reading Group. So it must have been in a strange language. Maybe he would give it to me and Christopher and I could put it in our starship and say it was from another planet.

I heard a piece of metal. It was a broken spur. He threw out a tall furry hat, flat on top but meant to sit high on the head. I tried it on. It covered my ears and forehead and almost fell into my eyes. The fur had some bare patches on it, as if someone had pulled them out. It looked like it might be a nice warm hat to hike in. Only the kids might think it was funny and laugh.

"*Aha, Ochin Khorosho!*" said the Czar. He came out of the closet, kicked everything back in, and shut the door. The people in the nursing home must be afraid to tell him to clean up his closet. Benjie and I have to hang everything up at home and our shoes have to be in a straight line at the bottom of the closet.

The Czar held up a bottle of clear liquid and two tin glasses. He went over to the small sink in the room and rinsed out the glasses. "This, my good friend Joshua, is the vorld's finest Russian VODKA! Now if ve only had some delicious caviar." He showed me the crowns on the outside of the bottle. There was writing. It was in English. "'Suppliers to the Imperial Russian Court, 1886–1917.''

"Aha, my poor cousin Nicholas," he said. "He loved vodka, 'til the revolution, then—pouf." He poured a little into my glass and a lot into the other one. "But come now, this is time to celebrate your good luck."

I sniffed at the glass. There was no smell at all. The Czar said, "Vatch me, Joshua!" He held up the metal glass and took a big sip. He rolled it around in his mouth and then swallowed loudly with a large gulp. "Now your chance."

I took a sip. I really didn't taste anything. Maybe it was only water. I swished it around in my mouth and swallowed. Suddenly I felt a burning from the back of my throat into my mouth through my gums and onto my tongue. The burning even seemed to go up the back of my nose and make it curl just like from the paint smell.

I felt the sting even in back of my eyeballs. I opened my mouth for air.

"I need water. Please, WATER!" The Czar poured me water from the sink. I drank it quickly. It helped cool the burning inside my mouth, but now I felt the vodka making a warm path down the back of my throat into my stomach.

The Czar poured some more vodka into his own glass and drank it in a quick gulp. There was a knock on the door. I went to answer it.

"*Nyet!* Just a minute," whispered the Czar. He put the cork into the bottle of vodka and opened the closet. All the things came tumbling out again. He stood the bottle in the corner and kicked the clothes back into the closet. Than he pushed against the door 'til it shut. "O.K. Joshua, you may open door."

I opened the door. It was Mother. My eyes felt blurry as if I had been staring into the sun. I blinked a few times at her white uniform.

"Sorry, Mr. Romanoff, it's time for us to go. Joshua, why are you blinking like that?"

Mother noticed everything. I giggled a little. My head felt light, like it was filled with feathers. "Now Joshua, you have your lucky piece?" asked the Czar.

I put my hand in my pocket. I felt the winning half of the wishbone. "Yes, sir." I clicked my heels and saluted him.

"Joshua, what's the matter with you today?" Mother was looking very puzzled. She turned to the Czar. "I've been meaning to tell you, Mr. Romanoff, you really shouldn't wear such tight boots. It's not good for the circulation in your legs."

You could always learn medical stuff from Mother. The Czar clicked his heels and bowed to

Mother. "Thank you, dear lady, but vith these boots I led cavalry in a charge against Bolshevik revolutionaries in Kiev. I never give them up."

I have to remember that. Next time Mom tells me sneakers are bad for my feet, I'm going to tell her I won the world series in them.

"Well, Mr. Romanoff, make sure you lie with your legs up for awhile before you go to sleep."

"Thank you again, gracious lady, for advice."

Mother had the door open. "Let's go, Joshua." We walked out. The cardboard sign that said "Don't DESTERB!" was still hanging on the outside of the door. I took it off and handed it to the Czar.

"Mr. Romanoff, excuse me, but you spelled the sign wrong."

"Vat, vat are you saying?" I had forgotten how the Czar's voice could boom. But since my head was full of feathers, I didn't care. He didn't sound scary anymore.

"You spelled it wrong, Mr. Romanoff. It's 'Do Not Disturb!'"

"Are you sure, Joshua?"

I stood up straight and squared my shoulders. "Sure, I'm sure. I am a Super Power speller."

"You see," said the Czar. He slapped me on the shoulder. "It's vorking already." He gave me a big wink and shut the door.

"What's working, Joshua?" asked Mother. "What did Mr. Romanoff mean?"

A nurse's cart came rolling down the hall. I stepped to the side before Mother told me to watch out. It never even touched me.

"Oh nothing, Mother, just a special secret we have!"

# 12

I TRIED to talk to Mom on the way home but my eyelids kept falling down. She woke me when we were inside the garage.

"Honestly, Joshua, I don't know what's the matter with you today. You'd better go to bed early tonight."

I helped her set the table for supper. As I reached for some dinner plates I felt something sharp against my leg. I put my hand in my pocket and touched the chicken bone.

Mother was cutting up lettuce, tomatoes, green peppers, and cucumbers for salad. She couldn't wait for Dad to help, he was going to be late. Her words were as fast as her fingers.

"Joshua, are you listening to me?"

I nodded. She had been saying something about a party. I watched her slice the carrots. She cut one in half and handed it to me to eat. "Good for the eyes, Josh."

"Rabbit food!" I said. But I crunched it anyway. Christopher may think I should eat things that stick to my ribs, but right now I don't need a nickname like Jelly Belly. A few more big bites of carrot and that loose tooth might finally fall out. Mother was amazing. She didn't have one spot or sprinkle on her white uniform. If I tried to cut all those things up, my whole shirt would be splattered.

"Anyway," Mother said, "your friend Mr. Romanoff is going to be ninety years old on January 5 and Dr. Corby wants to have a big birthday party."

Ninety years old! Using my mathematical photographic brain . . . if I'm nine, almost nine and a half, that means the Czar is almost ten times older than me. He was eighty before I was ever born!

I said to Mother, "I don't know if the Czar would like a birthday party."

"Of course he would, Josh. Everybody likes a birthday party."

I don't, but I didn't want to tell her and make her feel bad. Every year she makes a big fuss over my birthday. I have to write a list of kids to invite and then think of a theme for the party. Either sports or cartoons or something like that. Then she buys invitations and tablecloths and napkins to match. One year when I was real little, the theme was the wild west. We had this dumb cowboy trying to lasso a bull across the top of the whipped cream icing. I wouldn't touch it. There were chocolate sprinkles on the edges and Benjie told me they were horse doo.

"Dr. Corby asked me to help arrange things and I'm stuck."

"What does he want you to do?"

"The refreshments are easy. The Home will make them. We'll have a big birthday cake with ninety candles. I called the newspaper and they're going to come take his picture."

"Oh, he'll like that." Even I'd like to get my picture in the paper. The Czar would probably stand with his riding stick, or maybe even the sword. Yes, that would be a great picture. "RUSSIAN CZAR LIVES TO AGE NINETY! SHOWN WITH SWORD THAT HE USED TO FIGHT HIS WAY OUT OF SIBERIA! HIS CLOSEST FRIEND IS JOSHUA WILSON!"

"And we have to have people at the party," she said.

"You've got Mrs. Horowitz and all those other old people."

"Yes, but they live there. Mr. Romanoff never has any visitors. He doesn't have any family."

I wanted to tell her that the Czar's whole family had been shot in the Russian Revolution. But Mom has ratings for things we're allowed to see and hear. Just like the movies. She'd probably think the Czar was telling R-rated stories, too much shooting.

"Of course our family will go, but I would like to have a lot of people help celebrate." Mother started mashing up potatoes. She poured in milk and butter. After she had gotten most of the lumps out she handed me the bowl and egg beater. Dad couldn't stand lumps in his potatoes. Mother said it was because of his stomach ulcer. He had to have food that was nice and smooth. Sometimes even certified public accountants have things go wrong. I whipped the potatoes into big hills with valleys in between.

"And entertainment. We've got to have entertainment. Josh, I was thinking about Christopher and his singing family."

I knew my mother wouldn't forget. Dad says she has a mind like a computer bank. Stores things up and ZAPS you with them. One of my potato mountains fell down.

"Do you think they would come and sing at the Home?"

I started mixing again. The swirls began to stand up stiffly. I had to admit it wasn't a bad idea. The Six C Notes would certainly be special entertainment at a party. Christopher told me they had matching costumes to wear when they sang. If

Mother didn't find entertainment, she'd make me play the piano. Mr. Wolfe had given me *The Gypsy's Tarantella*, but I only knew two lines by heart. Everybody's pretty sick of *The Spinning Song*.

"After all, Josh, the Czar is a real pal of yours. And being ninety deserves a special celebration."

These were the tallest mashed potato mountains I had ever made. Everything Mother said was right. There was only one problem. She sounded like she wanted me to ask Christopher to sing at the party. The mountain peaks started to sag again.

After supper, Benjie got out the weights. He'll probably make the Olympics someday, he never gives up. I had enough exercise today just breaking chicken bones.

"Move it, Josh. Time to work out!"

I looked at all the equipment. Benjie was jumping rope. I used to think only girls jumped rope, but Benjie showed me pictures of tennis players and fighters like Muhammad Ali in the sports magazines. They all jumped rope to build up their leg muscles.

"Pick up those barbells. Let's see if you can get to six tonight before you collapse."

I reached for the weights.

"Hurry," Benjie yelled. "I'm not doing this for my health, you know."

I felt for the chicken bone in my pocket. "Well, I'm not doing it for my health either."

"What did you say?"

I cleared my throat. Lucky I had gotten those mashed potatoes so creamy. There were no lumps in my stomach to start bobbing up and down.

"I already had gym today. And if the President of the United States has a physical fitness council that tells what a fourth grader should do, then that's all I'm doing."

I walked to the bathroom—quickly. Just in case Benjie took it the wrong way and decided to rearrange my ears or nose. "You know something, Benjie. I never told you before. I hate to lift weights." I closed the door. And waited. I ran the water and flushed the toilet. Just to make some noise. It was quiet. I opened the door and poked my head out. Benjie was still standing there with his hands on his hips. "But I like to watch you lift. You go ahead, and I'll learn by watching."

"You're never going to have muscles, you know that? But O.K., if you want to be a weakling that's your business. I'll let you watch the pro tonight." He shook his head like he was real disgusted with me but soon he was trying to jump to three hundred without missing.

"Phone, Josh," Dad called from the den.

It was Christopher. His voice sounded funny. "I can't hear you too good, Chris."

"I can't play on Thursday. You know, to work on the starship."

"What did you say?" He must have his hands across his mouth.

"We have to sing Thursday at the Elks dinner. My mother just told me."

"The Elks? Where's the dinner going to be, at the zoo?" I laughed at my own joke.

"Ha, ha," said Christopher. There was a click on his end.

"Dear sweetie baby brother, you better get off the phone."

"I just got on the phone!"

"Who's that?" I asked.

"Carol." There was another click.

"Are you still on that phone, Christopher? I'm waiting to make a call."

"Oh no you don't, Clarissa," said Carol. "I'm next."

Christopher bellowed into the phone, "Will you both get off and let me finish? I've been waiting all night." There was another click.

"What's going on here? I have to make a telephone call." I figured that had to be Cindy. She was the only one not on an extension.

"You're the one who's been talking all night," said Clarissa.

"Well, I've got an assignment due tomorrow."

"Wilson, are you still on there?"

"Yeah, Christopher, I'm here."

"Stop interrupting us, Christopher, or I'm going to tell Mom," said Carol.

"Yeah, shut up and get off the phone, Christopher. You have all day to talk to your friends. As for you, Carol, if there's any telling, I'll do it," said Clarissa. "Now everybody hang up. You too, Cindy." Click. Click.

"Joshua?"

"Yeah, I'm still here." I wouldn't hang up for anything.

"Christopher, hang up!"

"Clarissa, I've got to tell Joshua something important."

"You have one minute."

"Anyway, Josh, we'll paint it next week. O.K.?"

"That doesn't sound important to me—you have thirty seconds."

"Sure. Don't worry." Maybe I could ask him real quick if he would sing for the Czar's party.

"You have fifteen seconds left."

"Oh shoot. See you in school, Wilson." Click.

"So long."

"Christopher has already hung up and I suggest you do too."

Click. Phew! This was no time to bug Christopher about singing again with those sisters.

I fell asleep right after my shower. Something

woke me in the middle of the night. I looked across at Benjie's bed. He was sleeping as usual with the pillow over his head. The clock glowed in the dark and said 2:30. I got out of bed quietly. It was cold on the floor but I ran into the bathroom. The laundry basket was still there. And so were the blue chino pants I had worn today. I stuck my hand in the pocket. The chicken bone was there. Was I lucky. Imagine having the chicken bone drown in the washing machine after I worked so hard to win it? I went back to bed and put it under my pillow. The clock said 2:34 and that's the last I remember until morning.

The class was all excited. Miss Garett and Mr. Magliore were giving out mimeographed sheets with instructions about our field trip to South Mountain Reservation.

Mr. Magliore was talking. "If you have canteens at home, fill them with water or juice for the hike."

Miss Garett continued. "The bus will drop us off on Pleasant Valley Way. Mr. Magliore has mapped out a trail. We'll hike for about an hour and then eat lunch in one of the open fields before starting back down."

Mr. Magliore and Miss Garett acted as excited as we did. They kept interrupting each other to give instructions. She was talking about safety. "Now it's very important for us to stay together."

"Yes." That was Mr. Magliore. "Sometimes the

trail gets very narrow. So we will use the buddy system."

"We don't want to choose for you," said Miss Garett. "So here's what we'll do." She pinned an empty white sheet on the bulletin board. "You may all pick your own buddies to walk with on the trail. By the end of the day please write your name and your buddy's name on this sheet."

The minute the class heard "buddy system," it started.

"Sue, be my buddy."

"Sure, Marjorie."

"Hey," yelled Peter Benson, "you and me, Andy."

"Right!" said Andy.

Miss Garett was still talking. "If at the end of the day there are any students who aren't matched up, Mr. Magliore and I will have to assign them to buddies."

Oh no. I better not fool around. In the third grade we had gone to the Statue of Liberty. I had to walk with the teacher because the class didn't come out even.

Should I ask Christopher? We were building a starship together. Maybe he wouldn't want to spend a whole day being buddies with me in front of the class. A pencil fell out of my drawer. I dropped to look for it and felt the sharp edge of the chicken bone through my pants. When I picked up my pencil I got out a piece of lined notebook paper. Miss Garett was writing vocabulary words on the blackboard.

I used my neatest lettering. I tried to make my o's really round. "Dear Christopher: Would you be my buddy Friday on the Field Trip? Sincerely yours, Joshua Wilson." I crossed out Wilson. I was the only Joshua in the class. I added a P.S. "We could decide what colors to paint our starship while we're walking along."

I wrote the note over because it didn't look too neat with the crossed out word. I used red ball point this time instead of pencil.

When I finished, I folded it up and walked over to the library table. I dropped the note on Christopher's desk as I walked by. Just the way all the kids pass notes. I tried to watch out of the corner of my eye as Christopher picked up the note and read it. Donald Schaffer leaned over and said something to Christopher. They laughed together. My heart slowed down and I thought about hiking with Miss Garett as my buddy.

Christopher scribbled something on the bottom. I couldn't tell if it was long enough to be YES or short enough to be NO! I walked back to my desk and waited.

Miss Garett called up Planetary Satellite One Reading Group to the front. Christopher was in that group. A tiny paper glider landed on my desk as he went by. It was the note. I opened it quickly. There were my words and on the bottom the secret Captain Future Space Code of dots and triangles that we learned from the magazines. I decoded it. Christopher's answer was "SURE!"

# 13

Field trip! Today I was glad the sun was shining and that New Jersey was having the warmest December in its whole entire history. The weatherman had said so on the news last night. I zipped the leg zippers on my sweat suit. At last I finally had something to warm-up for. Mom handed me an old gray sweatshirt of Benjie's. "Take this with you. It's supposed to get cooler."

I didn't argue because she always wins when it comes to sweaters and boots. "Your lunch is in the brown paper bag in the refrigerator. I filled Benjie's canteen with apple juice. It's on the counter."

I got the brown paper bag and put the canteen over my shoulder. I opened the bag and stuck my nose inside. Ah, tuna fish. Good. Mom was tying her bathrobe. "Don't you want some breakfast?"

"No thanks. I had juice, that's enough."

"Yes, but you're going to be hiking. At least take a piece of bread with peanut butter."

I let her win with the sweatshirt, but I couldn't stuff a thing down my throat, I was too excited. "I've got to meet Christopher."

"O.K. Josh. Have a good day."

It looked like every kid in the schoolyard had on a gray sweatshirt. I looked for the biggest one and there was Christopher. He had two canteens, one over each shoulder. He tapped them. "This is Hawaiian Punch and this one's Gator Ade."

"How was your show last night?"

"Shh." Christopher pulled me around the shoulders. "You know, I don't want those other kids to know." He shook his canteens. "But we were pretty good. We had two encores."

"What's an encore?"

"That's when they like you so much, they clap and stamp their feet until you sing the song all over again."

I had had an encore with *The Spinning Song* and didn't even know it.

Mr. Magliore blew his whistle. He had on a gray sweatshirt with Deerfield School printed on it in black letters. Miss Garett was wearing dungarees, but she had on a bright red sweater that buttoned all the way to her chin and a red wool hat pulled over her ears.

"Line up with your buddies." Mr. Magloire was going to run out of breath today blowing that whistle.

It was a quick ride. When the bus stopped, we jumped off and started chasing each other across the wide open field. The whistle blew again. And again. "Buddies! Everybody together." Miss Garett was holding her hands around her mouth like a cup, so her voice could come out louder.

Mr. Magliore gave more instructions. We would walk two by two up the trail that began with a clump of giant oak trees. At first, the climb would be easy. But then Mr. Magliore told us it would get steeper and steeper. We must stay on the trail and of course stay with our buddies.

Miss Garett gave us a science sheet. We had to gather four samples of leaves and seeds from the oak, evergreen, maple, and honey locust. She gave us plastic bags to hold our samples in.

We started off. Marjorie and Sue were first, then Christopher and I and Peter Benson and Andy.

"Oh look, an acorn." Marjorie bent down and the rest of us had to stop.

Peter Benson started yelling. "C'mon, Marjorie, you're not supposed to stop so soon."

We walked a few steps more. "I see some pine

cones." Marjorie ran into the evergreen bushes. We had to stop again. This time Christopher spoke up. "Hey, Marjorie, let us go ahead of you, if you're going to stop every five minutes."

"Maybe we should get our pine cones too, Chris?" I asked.

"Naw, we just started. Way up on top of the trail, that's where we'll find the really good stuff."

We started off again. Christopher took a drink of Hawaiian Punch. He wiped his mouth with the back of his hand. He had a big purple mustache left on his lip.

I took a swig of apple juice, even though I really wasn't thirsty. My morning orange juice was still sloshing around in my stomach. I wiped my mouth the same way Christopher had. Apple juice doesn't leave a good mustache.

Christopher peeled a banana. Somebody in the back of the line started singing, "This old man, he played one, he played knick, knack on my thumb . . ." The song moved up the line and soon we joined in. "Knick, knack, patty wack, give your dog a bone, this old man came rolling home . . ."

I sang as loud as I could. But I listened with one ear. Christopher had a real strong voice. I could see how the Elks would ask for an encore. He started on one of his sandwiches. "Hiking makes me hungry," he said.

There was a little bit of a breeze and sometimes

a leaf or branch would reach out and tickle my cheek or nose. The sun was shining and you could hear our feet crackle the twigs in time to the music. Every once in awhile, Christopher and I would bump shoulders. He was eating Fig Newtons. I felt for the chicken bone in my pocket. This is how the Czar must have felt when he marched with his men while looking for Markovo. Before his toe got frostbitten and zapped off, of course.

We got to a large open grassy field about 11:30. Mr. Magliore blew his whistle. "Lunchtime."

We sat on the grass and tore open our lunch bags. Miss Garett cupped her mouth again. "Don't forget to clean up when you're through."

I sat down. Christopher looked in his paper bag, rolled it up, and threw it on the ground. He had eaten everything while climbing the trail.

I picked up the bag and put it with my own garbage. "Hey, Christopher, want half a sandwich? My mother packed too much for me."

"Yeah, thanks, Wilson." Christopher reached out for the sandwich. Marjorie gave one of her loud whispers. "Look at Mr. Magliore and Miss Garett." They were sharing drinks from the same canteen. Marjorie and Sue were hysterical laughing. "She's giving him a bite of her apple," said Marjorie. "Love!" squealed Sue. "Germs!" I whispered to Christopher.

Christopher gulped down the last bite of tuna

fish. "We should try to get our tree samples now, Wilson."

"O.K." I tried to chew a little faster to catch up. I split my Hostess Cupcakes with Christopher, even though he had eaten his own two packs on the way up.

"Boy, thanks, Joshua. It's pretty good having you for a buddy. Your mother makes a good lunch."

I broke off some grapes from my bunch and handed them to him. Maybe I could ask him to sing at the Czar's party. If Christopher knew about the birthday cake and other refreshments he might want to go. But before I could swallow my grapes quickly enough to talk, Christopher was on his feet.

Peter Benson went over to ask Mr. Magliore if he and Andy could start looking for their tree samples. Mr. Magliore stood up. "Peter, you and Andy and Christopher and Joshua and Marjorie and Sue will be one group. Stay together. We'll be sitting right here. Don't go deep into the woods." He showed us the trees that were all around the field. "Yes," said Miss Garett, "you should be able to get all four samples from the trees at the edge of the field."

Christopher growled in the back of his throat. "Why do we have to get stuck with Marjorie again?" Marjorie heard him.

"Never mind," she shouted back. "Who wants to be with you and your klutz friend over there?"

I wonder if tongues ever get frostbite.

The six of us walked off together with Christopher leading. Marjorie tried to get ahead but Christopher just walked faster. I had to run to keep up. Lucky my body was in such good condition.

When we reached the edge of the field, Sue pointed ahead to some evergreen bushes. "Oh look, there's some beautiful pine cones." When we got to the bushes, Peter Benson spotted some large oaks farther up and a little off the trail. "Let's go," he yelled.

I looked back. The trees had closed around us and you couldn't see the field anymore. But you could still hear kids and Mr. Magliore's whistle.

From the oak trees we moved farther up the trail. "Miss Garett said we were to stay in the woods on the edge of the field," I told the kids.

"Do you think we're going to get lost?" asked Peter Benson. Marjorie and Sue pushed each other and Marjorie said, "What do you expect from the Klutz?"

Even Christopher kept walking. "C'mon, Josh, the trail is right here. Gee whiz, you can't get lost in the South Mountain Reservation. We're right in the middle of New Jersey. We didn't leave civilization."

"Look at the pods on that tree." Sue pointed to

the branches of a tall honey locust. There were long green pods that looked like string beans hanging from the branches.

"Those are the seeds," yelled Andy.

"Let's try to get them." Peter Benson tried to reach but the branches were up too high. Christopher tried next and then the two girls. I sat on a rock.

"Why don't we get a stick and knock them off?" Marjorie picked up a crooked branch from the ground and started swinging at the tree. She still couldn't reach.

"Let's look around the ground. Maybe some of those pods fell off," I said.

"Oh that's no good. The pods on the ground are all crumpled and dried out." Marjorie turned to Sue. "Isn't that right?"

"Yeah, we want those fresh green ones from the tree."

Christopher called Peter Benson and Andy. "Help me pile up those rocks." We rolled three large rocks together and the girls found a fourth. Piled together, the rocks made a little stepladder to walk on. "I'll get them now." Christopher walked up the rocks and balanced himself.

"Be careful, Christopher," I said. Those rocks were pretty wobbly.

Christopher still couldn't reach a branch so he

called to Marjorie, "Hand me that stick." Christopher hit the stick against one of the branches. Two pods and some leaves fell down.

Sue scooped them up.

"Now get some for Peter and me," Andy said.

Christopher hit the tree again. This time three pods fell down along with a bunch of leaves.

"That's enough, Christopher, come on, let's go." I wanted him to stop but he was still swinging that stick. There was a clump of pods hanging from a side branch. Christopher pointed to them. "Those are for us, Josh."

I watched him stretch up on his toes at the same time the rocks started to roll apart. For one instant Christopher was left swinging the stick at the tree branch before his feet fell off the slipping rocks and he tumbled to the ground.

He fell on his right side and lay there all crumpled up. Nobody spoke. We just stared at him.

Marjorie moved first. "Christopher, Christopher, are you all right?" She moved over to shake his shoulder. He didn't answer. She started to cry and shook him harder. "Christopher, Christopher!" Sue sat down on a rock and hid her face in her hands. Peter Benson and Andy just stood there, the green pods still in their hands.

I felt like my feet were glued to the ground. I should have climbed for the pods. Christopher was just too fat for those rocks. And I'd made him fatter by giving him half my lunch. I swallowed hard. All I could see was his crumpled-up body. A leaf fell off the tree with two green pods. They landed on Christopher's shoulder.

# 14

CHRISTOPHER STARTED to moan. Softly at first, then louder, "Oh my head, my head."

My legs began to work. So did my arms and I opened my mouth. "Marjorie! Marjorie, don't shake him. If his head's hurt, we can't move him."

Marjorie looked up. Her hand was still on Christopher's shoulder. Her nose was running and her shoulders were shaking. One part of my photographic mind noticed that she looked pretty gross.

I shook her. "Stop crying. That won't help him." I bent down next to Christopher. "It's O.K., Christopher. I'm going to see where you're hurt." I looked at his head and lifted up his hair. There was a big scrape where Christopher's head hit the ground. That's probably why he didn't answer us right away, he was knocked out. I got scared when I saw the blood coming out of the scrape but I tried not to let the other kids know.

He was crying. "My foot, my foot. Oh, my foot." I lifted the bottom of his dungarees. The ankle that Christopher had fallen on looked like a baseball. It was swelling right through his sock and sneaker.

Marjorie and Sue were holding hands and crying. Peter Benson had a very red face. His cheeks were puffed out as if he were trying to hold back his tears. Andy was wiping his eyes and nose on his sleeve.

"Hey, c'mon everybody. We've got to help Christopher." I was trying to remember what Mom had told me about emergencies. "Marjorie, you're the fastest. You go get Mr. Magliore. Tell him Christopher fell and hurt his head and his ankle." Marjorie got up and started down the trail. I remembered the buddy system. "Hey, Peter." Peter had his head down. "Peter, you go with Marjorie. No one's supposed to be alone in the woods."

I watched Peter take off after Marjorie. Right now I wished that I was the fastest runner in the class. Christopher was starting to shiver. In between shivers he was crying.

"Christopher, don't worry." I unzipped my gray sweatshirt. Mom had been right about it getting cold. But she didn't know I'd need it to keep

Christopher warm. "Andy, you and Sue give me your sweatshirts."

The two of them pulled off their shirts. Even though the sun was out, it was cool in the woods where the tall trees blocked out the sun's rays. The ground must be freezing. Christopher's teeth were making noise as they rattled against each other. I kept talking as I covered him with the three sweatshirts. I wrapped them as tight as I could.

"Christopher, you're all right. You're fine. Just stay still and Mr. Magliore will be here in a minute." I checked his head. It was just bleeding a little bit. I took a tissue from my pocket and wiped the blood off as best as I could.

Christopher's shivers stopped but he was still crying. "Josh, my leg hurts, oh my foot, I can't move it."

"Don't move it, Christopher. Don't worry, you're going to be fine."

He was quiet for a minute, then he started again. "What if my leg is broken? What if they can't fix it? My mother'll kill me. Oh, it hurts."

"Your mother won't kill you. As a matter of fact . . ." I bent over and whispered in his ear so Sue and Andy wouldn't hear. ". . . this is probably good for two Captain Future laser guns at least."

"Do you think so?"

"Sure. And it's only your ankle. When my

mother worked in the hospital she used to tell me about some legs that were all broken in parts and had pieces of bone sticking out. Yours isn't anything like that."

He tried to raise his head to look. "Are you sure?"

"Of course I'm sure. Ask Sue. Ask Andy." I called them over. "You don't see any pieces of bone sticking out of Christopher's leg, do you?"

Sue looked like she was going to gag. Andy bent over Christopher's leg. "Joshua's right, Christopher. There isn't one piece of bone sticking up. Here." Andy handed Christopher the two pods that were on his shoulder. "Take these, Christopher. I bet you'll have the best science specimens in the whole class."

We heard Mr. Magliore's whistle and saw him follow Marjorie and Peter Benson up the trail. Mr. Magliore could stand and blow that whistle in my ear for the next five hundred years, I was so happy to hear it.

He took a good look at Christopher's head and ankle. He patted me on the back. "Nice work, Josh. You're a real take-charge guy when the chips are down!"

Things started happening real fast after that. I tried to stand up and found that my legs were shaking. Like I had run a five-mile race. My kneecaps were knocking against each other. I had to grab each leg tightly and hold on until the shaking stopped.

Miss Garett had gone down the road to call an ambulance and soon the first aid squad was there. Mr. Magliore took his own sweatshirt off and wrapped it around Christopher's ankle like a pillow.

When Christopher saw the first aid squad and the stretcher he started to cry again. I tried to calm him. "It's only the first aid, Christopher. They'll give you a real neat ride to the hospital."

Christopher was lifted onto the stretcher. The first aid team put cold packs on his ankle. "I want Joshua to go with me," Christopher cried out. The lady captain of the squad looked around. "Which one is Joshua?"

"I am."

"Well come on. One person is allowed to ride with the patient. If he wants you, then you're the one."

I looked at Mr. Magliore who nodded yes. "You go ahead, Joshua. We'll call your mother and meet you at the hospital."

The ride to the hospital went too quickly. The squad made Christopher comfortable and he stopped crying. The lady driver put the siren on for us and showed us the different signals for turning corners and going through lights.

We passed the school and I wondered whether anyone could see me riding with Christopher in the back of the ambulance.

His mother was waiting at the hospital. So were Clarissa, Cindy, and Carol. Miss Garett must have called them.

His stretcher was wheeled toward the emergency room. I figured he'd take one look at his sisters and wish he was knocked out again.

His mother leaned over the stretcher. "How are you, honey?"

"My ankle's killing me . . ." and he started to cry all over again. It's funny, sometimes you can hold back crying for a long time when you're with strangers. Then when your mother and father come around you don't have to be brave anymore. His sisters came around the stretcher but they didn't say a word. A nurse tried to move them away. As soon as Clarissa was pushed out, Cindy moved closer. When another nurse sent Cindy to the waiting room, Carol popped up on the other side of the stretcher. The nurses were getting mixed up. "I thought I just sent you out of the room?" one asked Carol.

I answered. "No, you sent her sister. They're twins."

The doctor came and made all of us leave the emergency room except for Christopher's mother.

"Poor Christopher," said Clarissa.

"He looked so pale," said Carol.

"Oh just let him be all right and I swear, I'll never tease him again," cried Cindy.

They sat on a leather couch and held hands. I don't think they even noticed me. Finally Mr. Magliore walked in. "How's Christopher?" he asked.

I shook my head and nodded toward the closed door. "He's in there with the doctor."

I pointed to the couch where the girls were. "Those are his sisters." Mr. Magliore walked over to them. "Hello girls, I'm Mr. Magliore. Don't worry, I'm sure Christopher will be fine."

They just shook their heads and stared at the floor. There was a candy machine in the corner. I wished they would eat something or jump around or even sing. Anything but sit there so quietly.

Mr. Magliore tried to smile at me over their heads. He was worried too. It wasn't his big winking smile.

Christopher's mother came out of the examining room. She saw Mr. Magliore. "Oh Mr. Magliore, Chris is all right. He has a slight concussion from the fall and a fractured ankle. They're putting a cast on now and then we can take him home. He'll have to rest for a few days and he'll be on crutches for at least four weeks."

My legs started to shake again and I felt an ache between my shoulders where I had been holding myself straight and tight. This time I let my legs shake. Christopher was going to be all right. And crutches! Maybe Christopher wouldn't think so, but I thought it was pretty neat. Four weeks with no gym and by that time we were sure to have snow and all the softball playing would be over.

Christopher's mother smiled at Mr. Magliore. "I want to thank you for calling so quickly and taking care of Chris until the ambulance came."

The wrinkles in Mr. Magliore's forehead had straightened out when he heard the good news. He had his regular big smile as he shook her hand.

"I'm not the one you should thank." He put his hand on my shoulder. "Here's the young man who sent for help and kept Chris quiet and comfortable until the ambulance came."

It was very quiet in the waiting room. Then Christopher's mother put her hands on my shoulders. The pressure made me look up into her eyes. "I just want you to know, Joshua, that I am proud that Christopher has such a wonderful, self-reliant boy for a friend."

I felt a nice warm tingle from my head to my toes. It made me stand straighter and taller. It was like hitting a home run with the bases loaded. Though I really don't know how that feels since I've never done it.

"Hey, aren't you the kid that was playing at our house a couple of weeks ago?" asked Cindy.

"Yeah."

"What's your name again?"

"Joshua."

"Put it there, Josh." She shook my right hand, Carol grabbed my left. Clarissa waited until they were finished and then she shook both my hands together.

Cindy reached for Clarissa's shoulder bag. "Got any change? There's a soda machine in the corner, I'm just about to die of thirst."

"For me too, Clarissa, and a candy bar. I need some quick energy. I was just about to faint from nerves," said Carol.

"How about you, Joshua, can we get you something?" asked Clarissa.

I shook my head no and watched the girls move over to the machines. Christopher hadn't been hurt long enough for them to lose even one ounce.

Mr. Magliore ruffled my hair, just like Dad does when I do something that makes him happy.

"Well, Josh, I better be driving you home before your mom starts to worry." Mr. Magliore shook hands again with Christopher's mother and steered me to the door. The girls yelled, "So long." Christopher's mother called out, "I'm going to phone your mother, Joshua, to tell her how proud she should be of you."

Mom was waiting outside as we pulled up. When I got out of the car, she grabbed me and gave me a tight hug and kiss. She looked me over carefully. "Are you all right?"

"Sure, Mom, I'm fine. I didn't get hurt. Christopher did."

She gave me an extra hug anyway. Christopher's right. Mothers do go bananas when they think their kids are hurt.

She walked over to the car window to shake hands with Mr. Magliore. "Thanks for bringing Joshua home."

"Oh I was happy to, Mrs. Wilson. We're really proud of your son."

Mother hugged me again. "So are we, Mr. Magliore. But then we've always been proud of Joshua."

Mr. Magliore waved out the window. "See you in school on Monday, Josh."

"O.K., Mr. Magliore." I waved back.

Mother and I walked into the house. She gave me a glass of milk and some cookies. I was really hungry and even though it was backwards I asked Mom to fix me a peanut butter and jelly sandwich after I ate the cookies. It was hard to remember back to this morning and the hike and eating lunch on the trail. So much had happened.

I went to take a shower. I took off my pants and got ready to throw them in the dirty laundry basket. I put my hand in the pocket to pull out my chicken wishbone, but it wasn't there. I searched the other pocket and my sweatshirt. I even looked to see if it had gotten caught in my shoes or socks. My heart was thumping as I shook everything out. I remembered feeling the wishbone when we were marching. It must have fallen when I pulled the tissues out of my pocket to wipe Christopher's head.

I started to feel a little scared about losing my good luck charm. I had promised to carry it with me all the time. But I thought of the Czar, his face serious and his booming voice yelling out, "PPPPPPPPPPPPPPUUUUUUUUULLLLLLLL . . ."

And that made me smile. I started to whistle the way Benjie does when his team wins a soccer game. If I could get the winning half of the wishbone once, why I guess I could just do it again!

# 15

I RESTED up real good over the weekend. Mom
made French toast on Saturday and Dad made me
waffles on Sunday. And nobody told me that too
much maple syrup was bad for my teeth. Even
Benjie didn't yell at me until Sunday night and
then he just said, "Don't use my colored pencils
without permission."

I called Christopher. "How are you feeling?"

"Pretty good, Josh. Guess what?"

"What?"

"My mother bought me a complete new set of
model paints. So we can finish our starship."

"Neat! Next week's Christmas vacation so we
can work on it."

"You'll have to come here. I can't walk. Because of my cast."

"That's O.K."

"And my sisters chipped in and bought me a poster of Captain Future."

"That's great."

"And my father has a friend who has a cousin who knows Joe Namath. And he's trying to get him to sign my cast."

"That'll be terrific."

"Yeah, but the guy says you usually have to be dying, because these big stars don't have time to visit people that are going to keep living."

"Well, maybe if Joe can't come out to your house and sign it, you can send it to him. When the doctor takes it off. Then he can send it back and you'll still have his autograph for a souvenir."

"Sounds a little complicated that way."

"Sorr-ee, your FIVE minutes are up!"

"Who's that, Chris?"

"It's Carol. We have a new system with the phones in our house."

"Your FIVE minutes are up!"

"My father put egg timers next to the extensions. You flip them over and can talk for five minutes. Then you have to hang up and make your call again—later."

"O.K., I'll see you next week."

"O.K. I'll be watching Captain Future reruns in

the morning while you're having math. Ha, ha."

"Ha, ha, yourself! You'll have all that home-work to make up."

We signed off.

The next day at school everybody made a big fuss over me. Even kids from other classes had heard about Christopher's accident. After opening exercises Miss Garett wrote my name on the black-board. "Joshua Wilson, good citizen of the month from Room 227."

Marjorie walked over to my desk during study period. "Hey, I want to tell you something." I had been drawing a get-well starship for Christopher. The kids around me got so quiet, I knew they were trying to listen. Her face got red as she looked around the class. "I'm sorry I called you Klutz on the field trip. It just slipped out. I mean you're really not a klutz, except when you play softball. But you could even be on my team next time. If you don't try to catch any balls. I mean you could be the first aid director. Nobody's perfect. You know what I mean."

Maybe it wasn't Marjorie who called me on the phone. I always knew she told you things right to your face. Anyway my photographic memory gave me a zap and I remembered how she looked crying in the woods and with her nose running.

"That's O.K., Marjorie."

She took one deep breath. "Joshua-would-you-be-my-partner-in-spelling-I-know-you're-Chris-topher's-partner-but-maybe-just-until-he-comes-back. I've just got to get out of Blast Off!"

I counted my colored pencils. Peter Benson leaned across the desk. "Boy, Wilson, why don't you tell her to take a flying leap in the garbage heap?" Then he must have remembered how she acted on the field trip. He turned to the other kids and said, "You should have seen Marjorie crying when Christopher got hurt." He pointed to her. His voice started low and then got louder. "Baby, baby, stick your head in gravy. . . ." The other kids joined in. ". . . Wash it out in bubblegum and send it to the navy. . . ." They all giggled. Even Sue was flopping all over her desk in hys-terics.

Marjorie started sniffling like she had a bad cold, but her eyes looked like they were going to start to cry. Too bad she hadn't remembered how dumb Peter Benson had acted first!

Miss Garett rapped on her desk for quiet. "What's going on, class? What are you singing back there?"

"I'll do spelling with you, Marjorie," I said. "But only until Christopher comes back to school."

Marjorie went back to her desk to get her spell-ing book. She pulled a rolled-up dirty tissue out of her drawer. As she passed Peter Benson's desk, I could hear the teasing song start again. "Baby, baby, stick your head in gravy. . . ."

The week went by quickly. I couldn't visit the Czar on Tuesday because Benjie had an emergency dentist appointment. I was kind of worried. His party was supposed to be next week and Mother hadn't said anymore about it. I couldn't ask Christopher to sing, because his leg was in a cast. And he had a bald spot in his hair, where the doctor had to shave him to stitch the cut. Christopher had laughed about it. "The doctor said he was going to sew 'Souvenir of Fourth Grade Field Trip' right in the middle of my head!"

I thought that would be a pretty neat trick if he could do it.

I asked Mother about the party at dinner. "Oh don't worry, Joshua. So much has happened in the last couple of weeks. Our family will go and the Home will make delicious refreshments. It will work out fine."

I wasn't so sure. I tried to write a special poem for the Czar but each time I crossed out more words than I wrote.

Mother asked what I would like to give him for a present. Everyone tried to be helpful. Even Benjie. "Why don't you give him a tie?"

I thought of the special shirts he wore. "No, he doesn't wear ties."

Dad said, "Maybe there's something special he likes to eat or drink?" I remembered the bottle of vodka in the bottom of the closet. Somehow I didn't think the Czar would want anyone to know about that.

Benjie tried again. "How about some aftershave lotion? You know, that gunk you slap on your face and then all the girls start to chase you."

"Very funny, Benjie. And you know he doesn't shave."

The day before Christmas vacation, Miss Garett had an apron on and her hair tied up. She made us clean out our drawers while she emptied the closets.

There was a stack of old books and papers on her desk. "I don't want to throw these out. So you can come up row by row and look through them. You may keep whatever you want and take it home."

Peter Benson, Marjorie, and Sue ran to the front of the room. Miss Garett slapped the desk. "I said row by row."

By the time my row was called there was hardly anything left.

"Ah, there's just some junky old maps here," said Andy. "If I bring anything more home, my mother'll throw me out."

"Yeah," said Peter Benson. "My mother says

that the Board of Health is going to condemn my room."

"Oh yeah," said Andy. "Well, my mother says my room is so full of stuff it's going to fall off the back of the house all by itself."

They went back to their seats. Everything was pretty dusty. I picked up the pile of maps. There was Africa and a small map of Denmark . . . and a map of Russia! And it was old. Because it was called Russia on the map, not the U.S.S.R.

"Can I have this, Miss Garett?"

"Sure, Joshua, just take it home with you."

I walked back to my seat. I asked Marjorie for a tissue and wiped the dust off. The colors were nice and clear. My hands were sweating. I looked for Siberia. There it was. And way up in the corner of the map I found it. IN RED LETTERS. Right next to a little stream. Markovo!

# 16

I COULDN'T wait to show it to everybody at dinner. Benjie grabbed it. "Let me see."

"Hey, Benjie, don't rip it."

"What do you know?" He showed it to Dad. "There really is a Markovo! So maybe your Czar really was a Czar!"

"I always told you he was."

Mother and Dad looked at the map and we all agreed. Dad would frame it in dark brown wood so the Czar could hang it in his room to show everyone that there was a Markovo.

"Uh, oh." I remembered my other picture. "They're not allowed to hang anything on the walls in the Home."

"No problem," said Dad. "I'll put a back on it and he can stand it on his dresser."

"Joshua," said Mom, "I think that will make a super present." I drew a picture of a tall man with a high fur hat on a big black horse all dressed for the winter snows of Siberia. I signed it: "Happy Birthday, to the Czar of Markovo, from your friend and fellow chicken bone wisher, Joshua Wilson and Family."

On January 5 we set out for the Home. It was just starting to snow and Mother was nervous. She yelled at Dad because he had forgotten to put snow tires on the car. Here I had been praying for snow since November and now it couldn't hold off one more day.

Mother had wrapped the map in blue paper with silver ribbons. I was happy about the present but I still wished that something more could have been done for the Czar. Maybe I should have tried harder to learn the last two lines of *The Gypsy's Tarantella*, since I didn't get The Six C Notes to sing.

It was quiet when we got to the front lobby. Dad hung our coats up on the rack. Benjie sniffed. "It smells funny in here." He sniffed again. I sniffed too. "It always smells like this," I told him. "You'll get used to it."

Mother led the way. "Come on. Everybody must be in the lounge. They've finished painting it."

The hallway was quiet. I guess the carts don't

roll at night. I hoped Benjie wasn't getting the wrong idea about the place. It isn't so creepy in the daytime. The only sound was our shoes clicking against the floor.

Dad opened the door to the lounge and Benjie pushed me into the room. I heard a big yell, "SURPRISE!" I looked around. "SURPRISE! SURPRISE!" Kids were screaming it. Someone was taking pictures and light bulbs were flashing in my eyes. "SURPRISE!" I tried to focus. Kids? Yeah, there was Peter Benson and Andy and Marjorie and Mr. Magliore and Miss Garett. Why, it looked like the whole fourth grade was here! The old people were sitting around a big table that was decorated with balloons and paper chains and had two cakes.

The present fell out of my hand. Some kids laughed and Peter Benson said, "Looks like Wilson thinks he's in centerfield."

Benjie picked it up. "I told you we shouldn't surprise him, the kid probably broke it."

"Quiet, Benjie." Dad shook the package. No sound of glass. "Don't worry, Josh, you didn't break it."

Mother turned me around. There was the Czar, dressed in the black silk blouse with red trim that I had seen on the bottom of his closet. It was pressed, his boots were shining, and his beard was combed into little curls. I was sure glad we hadn't bought him aftershave lotion.

The Czar stretched his hand out to me. "Thank you, my friend, for celebrating birthday vith me and bringing all your friends."

He clicked his heels together, then reached down and planted a large kiss on one side of my face and then on the other. He clicked again and saluted.

I turned to Mother. "But it's not my birthday."

She laughed. Miss Garett walked over. "You see, Josh," she said, "Christopher's family and the fourth grade wanted to do something special for you. Because of the way you took charge the day of the accident . . ."

I heard Peter Benson's loud whisper, "It wasn't my idea to do something special . . ."

"Mine either," said Andy. "I only came 'cause my mother made me."

"Shut up, you guys, or do I have to sit on you?" It was Christopher. He poked Andy with one of his crutches.

Now Mother was talking. "I told Christopher's mother and Miss Garett that you wanted to do something special for the Czar's birthday. We decided that the most special thing would be for both of you to celebrate together at one big party."

I heard a loud chord from the piano. And another; then two more. Pounding, like they do on TV when they introduce the President. There was Christopher's mother and father and Clarissa and

the twins. They were all dressed in matching singing costumes. Looked like I was finally going to
hear The Six C Notes. But Christopher didn't have
a costume on. Before I could ask him why, he
pulled me to the side.

"Listen, Wilson, it's The FIVE C Notes tonight—get it—FIVE! If it was just the old guys I
wouldn't care, but I wouldn't sing in front of these
kids even for you." He tapped his cast with a
crutch. "Lucky my ankle's broken. I told my mom
that I wouldn't be able to sing on key because I'm
all off balance."

Well, even Five C Notes were a big surprise. I
hadn't expected any! I promised I wouldn't say
anything about him being part of the group and
we shook on it.

The Czar grabbed my shoulder. "Enough of
this. Ve have things ve discuss."

"First the cake, Mr. Romanoff!" It was Mrs.
Horowitz. I was surprised that she talked back to
him. She led me to the table. There was a yellow
and white cake. It said, "Good work, Joshua." On
the other end was a blue and white cake. It said,
"Happy Birthday, Mr. Czar." I should have told
them to make his cake with purple icing, because
purple's the royal color. The cakes were covered
with lit candles.

"Hurry up, Josh, blow them out so we can cut
up the cake," said Christopher.

"Yeah, hurry," Marjorie called out. Then in a lower voice I heard her say to Sue, "That's the only reason I came—refreshments!" It's funny how I always manage to hear kids say something about me even when they're supposed to be whispering.

The Czar stood by his cake. "Now ve both take big breaths, Joshua. Remember, ve got another chance for good vishes."

"I hope it's chocolate inside," a voice called out. I didn't have to look. I knew it was one of Christopher's sisters.

The Five C Notes started singing. "Happy Birthday and Thank You, Josh, Happy Birthday and Thank You, Josh. . . ."

I think Christopher's a C Note whether he wants to be or not, because he was standing next to me and his crutches were tapping in time to the music. He really had kept this party a secret. All the time we worked on our starship over vacation, he never said a word.

I gave the Czar his present. He tore off the ribbons and paper. He held the framed map up for everyone to see. I pointed to Markovo. "Look, Mr. Romanoff. Look. Here on the map. It's Markovo!"

Even Dr. Corby came over for a look. The Czar nodded. "So it is. Vell. No vonder I never find it. I came to that river but it vas cold and Sasha never like to get feet wet."

"Who's Sasha?" asked Marjorie.

"Sasha! Sasha!" The Czar boomed out. He didn't have his riding stick handy or I'm sure he would have cracked the floor. Marjorie jumped from his voice. "Sasha vas my very dearest friend and most vonderful horse, from whom I vould never part."

Marjorie turned away. "Pooh," she said and this time she didn't bother to whisper. "I don't believe it and anyway that's just an old map that Miss Garett was throwing away when she cleaned out her closets. Nobody else in the class wanted it but Joshua."

I know the Czar heard. Everybody heard, she talked so loud. Mrs. Horowitz spoke to her. "Come here, dear. What's your name? Marjorie? I don't think I showed you the picture of my grandson." And, frail and wrinkled as she was, Mrs. Horowitz pulled Marjorie to the other side of the room.

The Czar bowed to everybody and then to me. "I thank you again, dear friend, and vill alvays treasure map as token of our friendship."

"Refreshments!" yelled Mr. Magliore and everybody made a run for the table. Christopher's mother called out to the girls, "Be careful of your costumes, we still have some singing to do."

"Come on, Josh, Mr. Romanoff." Mother was holding out two plates. "Have some cake."

The Czar clicked his heels and bowed to her. "Lovely lady, ve thank you, but Joshua and I have special business to attend." He waved to the room. "All of you—EAT! Ve be back. Then ve listen to music. My riding stick, please."

Benjie found the stick. "Can I go with you?" he asked. The Czar didn't let me answer. "Ve sorry, Benjie. Vait vith others, ve be right back. Come, Joshua."

Mother was left standing with the two plates of cake. I just shrugged my shoulders at her as I followed the Czar out the door.

"Ah lovely lady, your mother. She reminds me of my dear beloved Princess Olga."

"Who?" I asked.

He thumped the riding stick on the floor. "You mean never I tell you about beautiful Princess Olga and how I sold Sasha for to help her escape over mountains?"

"No, I never heard about Princess Olga. You sold Sasha? You just said you would never part with her."

We reached his room. The Czar sighed. "Yes, I did. My beautiful Sasha for my beautiful Olga. But it's long sad story. Ve go inside and I tell about it."

I opened the door. The Czar sat on the bed. "First, Joshua, open closet and bring out special bottle of refreshment. Friends like us need vun private toast." He reached for a dried wishbone from the window sill. "Now ve see. If they lucky ve go back to party . . ."

I wiped my hand on my pants só it wouldn't be sweaty and I wiggled my thumb back and forth to loosen it up before I put it on half the wishbone.

"Ready?" he asked.

"Ready!"

"O.K. Vun, two, three, PPPPPPPPPPPUUUUUUUUU-UUUUUUUULLLLLLLLLLL. . . ."

## About the Author

Barbara Girion lives in Short Hills, New Jersey, with her husband and three children. A former teacher, she has been active in theater work and has developed scripts and education programs for both adults and children. Most of her story ideas come from real life. In *The Chicken Bone Wish*, she used her family's custom of breaking chicken bones and wishing. The story takes place at Deerfield School, which all of her children attended. The fabulous Czar whom Joshua meets is somewhat like Ms. Girion's Russian grandfather, who told fantastic stories of Siberia.